MW01077296

A
MOURNING
SONG

PRAISE FOR

A MOURNING SONG

BY MARK WESTMORELAND

"The wild ride of the rockabilly rollercoaster of the Dooley Brothers continues in *A Mourning Song*, where the fists swing wild and the shots go down smooth and the colors of the Southern landscape are dyed in shades of love, loss, and loyalty."
—**Michael Farris Smith**, author of *Nick* and *The Fighter*

"*A Mourning Song* is a jubilant addition to the New Southern Gothic canon. A lyrically electric trip down the dark and dusty back roads that take you through the heart of the South. Mark Westmoreland is quickly establishing himself as a writer to watch. Cousin, this dog can hunt!"
— **S.A. Cosby**, *NY Times* bestselling author of
Blacktop Wasteland and *Razorblade Tears*

"Mack Dooley, the narrator of A Mourning Song, is a haunted man, literally—his dead ex-girlfriend and the preacher who had her killed appear in increasingly disturbing visions that drive Mack to drink. As if that weren't enough, Mack's brother Marshall is missing, a white supremacist gang called the Ghostface Devils want to know where he is, and a war between the Devils and the local Bohannon crime family looms like a thunderhead over the north Georgia hills. A violent tale laced with humor and surprising lyricism, A violent tale laced with humor and surprising lyricism, *A Mourning Song* is a Southern Gothic noir as black as an abandoned church at midnight, with the promise of dawn hours away."
—**Christopher Swan**, author of *A Fire in the Night*

"The second installment in Mark Westmoreland's Dooley Brothers' series is a doozy. *A Mourning Song* plays perfectly off the final note of his first book (*A Violent Gospel*), belting out a raucous chorus of over-the-top, southern-fried crime. But don't let the shenanigans fool you. This book has heart. You won't make it past the final page without shedding a tear."

—**Eli Cranor**, author of ***Don't Know Tough***

"When we first see Mack Dooley in *A Mourning Song*, he's a mess of a man—haunted by a ghost, drunk half the time, yet still lovable as hell. Maybe it's his loyalty to his family or his violent morality or his determination to set things right when everything goes wrong, but his charm shines through even when he's crawling his way out of a bender. Mark Westmoreland has penned a worthy sequel to *A Violent Gospel*, and it stands alone as a kick-ass Southern story of remorse, revenge, and redemption. I, for one, can't get enough of those Dooley boys."

—**Tiffany Quay Tyson**, award-winning author of ***The Past is Never***

"Westmoreland's *A Morning Song* is deep-fried southern noir at its finest with equal parts brutal violence and tender yearning. Descriptions blast with sensory explosions one moment, then simmer with tension the next as the eldest Dooley brother reckons with his ghosts, both figurative and literal. Something tells me this won't be the last we'll see of the Dooleys. At least I sincerely hope not."

—**Heather Levy**, author of ***Walking Through Needles***

"Mark Westmoreland launched an absolute haymaker with his literary debut, *A Violent Gospel*, and with his stunning sequel, *A Mourning Song*, he follows up with a steel toe boot right to the teeth. Mack Dooley, as charming as he is hardheaded, now finds himself warding off the ghosts of his past while fighting the devils of his present. In this whiskey-soaked tale of revenge, family is everything, and law is whatever the Dooley brothers deem fit. Written with muscular, metaphoric prose, Westmoreland commands the page like a seasoned vet, further cementing his name alongside Southern noir's biggest names."

—**Scott Blackburn**, author of ***It Dies with You***

A
MOURNING
SONG

a Dooley Brothers novel

MARK
WESTMORELAND

SHOTGUN
HONEY
2022

A MOURNING SONG
Text copyright © 2022 **MARK WESTMORELAND**

All rights reserved. This book or any portion thereof may not be reproduced or used in any manner whatsoever without the express written permission of the publisher except for the use of brief quotations in a book review.

This book is a work of fiction. Names, characters, places, and incidents either are products of the author's imagination or are used fictitiously. Any resemblance to actual persons, living or dead, events, or locales is entirely coincidental.

Shotgun Honey
215 Loma Road
Charleston, WV 25314
www.ShotgunHoney.com

Cover Design by Bad Fido.

First Printing 2022.

ISBN-10: 1-956957-16-2
ISBN-13: 978-1-956957-16-7

9 8 7 6 5 4 3 2 1   22 21 20 19 18 17

For my friend Brooke,
Let your heart sing a new song

A MOURNING SONG

I believe every . . . man remembers the girl he thinks he should have married. She reappears to him in his lonely moments, or he sees her in the face of a young girl in the park, buying a snowball under an oak tree by the baseball diamond. But she belongs to back there, to somebody else, and that thought sometimes rends your heart in a way that you never share with anyone else.
  —James Lee Burke, *Black Cherry Blues*

"I'm gonna take, and take, and take, till they ain't got nothing left to give but blood . . . and I'm gonna take that, one drop at a time."
  —Buford Pusser, *Walking Tall (1973)*

DREAMS

Andrea Lewellen dances on the outskirts of my dreams, far away and out of reach.

I watch her spin and twirl, arms outstretched, eyes aimed toward Heaven. Her dress twists around her hips, and she beckons me to join her, speaking my name and tugging me forward into a timeless world where death and life have ceased and the restless linger.

We join hands, lacing our fingers together, and I loop an arm around her hips, pressing her body close to mine, and lead a Texas two-step. A divine rhythm guides and urges us on, and we move together as one, spinning and whipping across the Heavens, Andrea's ponytail lashing across her face. She becomes a whirlwind in my arms, gathering a band of wartime angles around us whose fists clutch lightning and hover with wings of fire.

They pry Andrea away from me, and, though I fight to keep her near, I do not belong here, lacking the strength I possess among the living. She slips from my hands, giggling at how the angels snatch her from her feet, her toes wiggling goodbye.

Andrea dances with the angels, streaking across a starless sky, obsidian in color and smothering. Her laughter trails after her the same way streams of fire tail the angels' wings. They lift her overhead, their arms rippling with the strain, their biceps and triceps defined slabs of muscles. She stretches out her arms, her hands catching the wind, almost providing her enough lift to fly on her own.

But a voice speaks.

It's trumpet-like and blares, blasting Andrea from flight, telling her she does not belong and must wait her turn. Her descent happens in a flash. She becomes a falling star, streaking across the obsidian-like sky, her celestial troupe powerless to save her. I struggle forward, fighting to reach her, my arms and legs pumping to gather the momentum required to dash to her aid.

She crashes before me.

The dream goes topsy-turvy, my knees wobble, and I cannot keep my balance, stumbling around like a drunkard, unable to answer Andrea's calls. A flash of light blinds me, my vision sears, and my sight goes snowy. Laughter fills my ears. It comes from all directions and pounds inside my chest, my heart rumbling along.

My legs give way, and I drop to my knees, kneeling like a man in prayer. I grind my palms into my eyes, kneading away the blindness, but I am not a physician and cannot cure myself. It is not until the laughter from all around coalesces before me, forming a figure I cannot see but can feel. The laughter reaches out, touches me, and a white hotness surges throughout my body, scalding my skin and scorching my bones, but my sight returns.

Randy Jessup looms above me.

He's tall and rail-like—a mile-long grin stretches across his face, full of capped teeth and laughter. Brother Jessup is wearing his Sunday best, a fitted suit the color of nighttime. His shoes shine, and he stares down at me with two working eyes. They're pale, almost translucent, and are the color of an early morning sky but cruel. He turns his gaze upon Andrea and leaves me where I kneel, unable to move or stop him.

Andrea flinches and attempts to retreat, but cannot flee, so she calls out to her angels, even hollers my name. A palpable fear emanates from her, and she shivers like a frightened child under the hand of an abusive parent. I fight to spring from my knees, but my wrists are shackled, my chains jangling and clinking as I jerk against them. I am bound to where Randy Jessup left me and can do nothing but watch.

Brother Jessup saunters over to Andrea, not in any rush or hurry, but once he reaches her, he moves all in a flash. She is in his arms and clothed in a new dress. It is not lively and beautiful like the one before—it is lifeless and drapes from her limbs. He leads her in a dance, slow and mournful, whirling her about without a care or concern. She cries in his arms, pounding her fists into his chest, struggling to tear away. He clutches her tighter, clasping his arms around her and squeezing until she claims she cannot breathe. Randy Jessup does not yield or let go. He spins faster and faster until they move at a tornadic beat, and he's lifted her above his head.

Andrea transforms before me. Her skin dries and peels away, leaving behind fresh scales. Her eyes blackout and become inky—possessed by a lifelessness that rends me. She becomes a copperhead in Brother Jessup's hands, and he jigs about, speaking in tongues and praising his Heavenly Father.

I scream and cry, hollering at myself to wake up, but I cannot force my soul from this dream. Its tentacles twist around my wrists and arms, binding me to it and forcing me to watch Randy Jessup minister and preach. He speaks in mysteries and parables, telling tales bestowed to him from another world. His words sap the life from me, draining me of all vitality, my hair falls out in clumps, and my teeth loosen in their gums. He grows more powerful and becomes a domineering figure, his voice full and booming, rattling my bones and shaking my spirit.

He laughs at the sight of me and laughs and laughs and keeps on laughing . . .

PART ONE

A FAMILY REUNION

1.

Heat lightning flickered across the Blue Ridge skyline, and a swarm of lightning bugs sparkled like the Dahlonega Christmas display Mama asked Deddy to go and see every chilly Thanksgiving weekend.

I sat in a rocking chair on my double-wide's redwood deck and had been sitting here so long I could feel the spindles leaving grooves upon my back. The evening air was so thick that it blanketed my arms and shoulders, glazing my skin with sweat. A bug zapper popped overhead, sending mosquitoes and fruit flies to whatever afterlife awaited them and grounded my mind in the present. I chugged straight from a bottle of Woodford Reserve, getting my brain swampy and in no condition for thinking.

This end-of-day routine had developed over the past year and a half, starting not long after I left Randy Jessup murdered in the basement of the Last Wave Revival Center, and got even more regular once Andrea Lewellen started haunting my dreams. Sleep did its best to evade me, punishing me with such severe insomnia that I went whole weeks without ever catching a wink. It made the alcohol necessary. Now, I had regular fights with my girlfriend about my drinking habits but slept here and there, though fitfully.

A pair of headlights blinded me when a car steered into my gravel drive. I shielded my eyes with a forearm and peered out, seeing Jessa behind the wheel. She waved at me, and I scrambled to hide the bourbon, shoving it behind a pot of geraniums, and rocked myself out of the chair.

The porch swayed beneath me, and the whole world went topsy-turvy until I laid a grip upon the banister, regaining my balance. I took my time descending the porch steps, each soft footfall more secure than before, and once I set a boot heel in the red Georgia clay, I no longer needed help keeping upright. Jessa swung her door open, and I leaned in for a kiss, trapping my tongue behind my teeth. If she tasted bourbon, it'd start a fight and ruin our night.

"Can you get them groceries out of the backseat?" She asked.

I stepped around her, opened the car's back door, and got the bags piled in the seat, twisting their handles around my wrists. Jessa used her hip to close her door and led me to the trailer. She wore a maxi dress with a blazing summer print, the fabric clinging to her hips and thighs, almost pasting to her skin. She'd French braided her hair into a ponytail that dangled down her back, allowing me to see pearls of sweat beading in the groove of her neck and shoulders. She walked up the steps in such a way I lost control of my eyes, and they swept back and forth in rhythm with the movement of her body.

Jessa held the screen door open for me, and I stopped to sneak one more kiss before going inside. We'd struck up this romance a little over a year ago, beginning it in the most peculiar ways, when she set eyes on me at a dive bar called Due South. Me and my brother, Marshall, were lying low at the time because of some money we'd stolen from this Pentecostal crime ring but needed to get out and breathe some fresh air before our stir craziness led us to yank a knot from each other's asses. I was keeping to myself that night, but Jessa ended up imposing her person upon me, and one thing led to another the way it sometimes does, and I spent the next three days locked inside a chest freezer.

Randy Jessup tortured me in cruel and various ways during that time, but once Jessa got to drowning in her guilt, she hunted my brother down and gave him the inside on where to find me. Behind the scenes, Marshall cut a deal with the Bohannon crime family, these sumbitches who got Deddy locked in Sweetwater State Penitentiary, and, with the help of Peanut and Caudell, Marshall got me free of Randy Jessup and his church.

It just so happened that my high school sweetheart, Andrea Lewellen, a girl I thought I would one day marry, got murdered at the hands of Randy Jessup after he dunked her in a baptismal tub full of vipers. I'd locked myself in my double-wide trailer to mourn her memory by drinking myself unconscious several weeks in a row. On one specific afternoon, Jessa stopped by the trailer, catching me before I swam to the bottom of a bottle of whiskey. After a fair amount of wariness on my part, Jessa explained why she helped the preacher entrap me and how she went about informing my brother of my whereabouts.

While Jessa explained her story, it occurred to me that it's always preferable to drink with company than to do it alone, especially if this company is an attractive young lady, so I invited Jessa inside. After a round or three of drinks, we shared what we said would be nothing more than a one-night stand, but here we are a year later, living together and agreeing that this is still nothing more than a one-night stand.

I dropped the bags on the kitchen table and sorted through everything Jessa got. She bought cotton balls, Q-tips, makeup wipes, toilet paper, moisturizer, body lotion, shampoo, hairspray, deodorant, toothpaste, and razors, but nothing to eat. I'd gone all day without having a bite, and my stomach grumbled for nourishment. The buzz whirling around the inside of my head got me heated, my skin prickled all over, and I squinted to keep from seeing two of Jessa. Before I could say something to irritate her mood, she spoke over me.

"I didn't grab nothing for supper cause I figured you could grill the venison Coach Cole gave us, or we could go out and grab a bite at Fat Mama's." She reached a hand out for mine, and the way she touched me cooled my temperature. "And I figured I could have you for dessert."

"Why don't we eat that first?" I said, pinning her against the counter and searching her body for my favorite parts.

"Cause I don't want you filling up on sweets."

"I got plenty of room for both."

Jessa smiled, and my temperature rose again, but not from anger; instead, she ignited a lust inside me, which caused my body to ache all over. "We start with dessert, and it'll ruin my appetite."

"Girl, you lie about as good as you look."

She pinched the back of my arm where the skin was extra sensitive and made me wince.

"Damn, Jessa," I said, massaging the pain from the muscle, "I meant you look good. You wear that dress just right."

"Go grill them steaks before you dig your hole any deeper."

I turned, got the meat out of the freezer, and opened the fridge. A twelve-pack of beer sat next to a half-gallon of milk and a two-liter of Coca-Cola. My taste buds yearned for another sip of booze, and my hand reached for a can unbidden. Jessa saw me try to hide it and stopped me from going out the backdoor.

"How much you done drunk tonight?"

No matter how much she tried to disguise her worry, she couldn't keep me from recognizing it in the tone of her voice.

"Don't start with me tonight, all right?"

"I wanna have a good night together, Mack."

Jessa only called me by my name when I did something to warrant her yelling at me, but she spoke in such a pitiful manner it got me angrier than if we got to hollering at one another.

"I'm gone have one beer, and that's all."

"Just one, please."

"What'd I say?"

I ignored how my tone made her smile falter and how doubt filled her eyes. It'd only get me mad to acknowledge what my behavior did to her, and I went outside alone. Moths flew around the yellow porch light, and cicadas buzzed a lonesome chorus. The humidity made the beer can sweat in my hand, and I rolled it across my forehead, its cool touch causing my anger to dissipate, and a guilty knot formed in my stomach. Without thinking, I rared back and flung the can the way Andruw Jones would hurl a baseball from deep center field. It flew end-over-end into the open-field next door and vanished into the summer evening.

Once I got the grill going, the steaks cooked fast, and I came back in the double-wide to find the kitchen empty. I sat the plate I carried on the counter next to a bowl full of steaming asparagus and went looking for Jessa, following the trail of clothes she'd left on the floor. She'd kicked her sandals off in the kitchen, left the maxi dress bunched up on the hallway floor, and her bra and underwear led me to the doorway of our bedroom. She'd curled up under a blanket, hiding her naked body from me.

Jessa teased me by spreading her legs beneath the comforter and began touching herself in ways that caused her hazel eyes to sparkle with heat lightning. A smile stretched across her face while she played, arousing an untempered lust within me, and I stepped across the threshold.

"I decided on having my dessert first."

"You sure you want them steaks getting cold?" I said, pointing a thumb over my shoulder.

"We can throw 'em in the microwave."

"You know I hate doing that." I undid my belt and started to yank it from the loops, but Jessa stopped me.

"Go slow for me," she said, pushing onto an elbow, almost breathless from pleasure.

I laughed and did what she asked, tossing my belt to her when I got it off. Jessa giggled, dropped it on the floor, and watched me shimmy out of my Levi's.

"Them girls at the Tattletale teach you that?"

"I've been saving that one for you." I tossed my shirt over my shoulder, crawled across the bed to Jessa's open arms, and fell into her embrace.

We kissed and generated the kind of heat only the steamiest Southern evenings can produce. She ran sharp nails up my back, a trail of gooseflesh pimpling along the ridge of my spine, and dug her fingers into my hair. Sweat beaded across my forehead, and the fading effects of the bourbon I drank earlier made my passions whirl around my brain.

We tussled around, getting tangled in the covers, struggling to get free of them, but once we finally did, we kicked them to the foot of the bed, coiled together, and stared into one another's eyes. Gray storm clouds swirled around Jessa's pupils, and her body tremored from the electricity kissing generated. Our passions swelled until I scooped an arm around her hips, positioning her near the edge of the bed. She opened her hips for me, and I slid between her thighs, grabbing a hold of the headboard the moment my soul got transported to another realm. I got lost inside Jessa, swimming deep into the pool of her, and did my best not to come up for another breath of air.

2.

ometime during the night, when my dreams of Andrea got the darkest, and I couldn't pry myself from the throes of terror, a hand clamped down over my mouth. I tried lunging upward, but my head got shoved into a pillow, and my eyes opened to see a hooded man standing over me, his face covered in tattoos, aiming a pistol at the bridge of my nose. He lifted the gun to his mouth and covered his lips with his trigger finger the way a librarian does when she means for a talking child to hush. I couldn't say a word anyway with his hand smothering me the way it was—the smell of reefer and swamp ass coated his skin and made me want to puke. He pointed the pistol barrel in Jessa's direction, and I looked over to see another man kneeling beside her, long hair covering the tattoos on his face, holding a knife to her throat. My balls got tight, and I clenched a handful of bedsheets, anchoring myself to the mattress.

The man peeled his hand away from my mouth when I didn't try fighting, allowing my lungs to fill with air uninfected by his turd-stained hands. He stepped away from my bed, crossed an index finger back over his lips, and used the gun to motion for me to get out of bed. I kicked my legs from under the covers and pushed myself off the mattress. The man kept his gun trained on me. He blended in with the shadows of my bedroom now and backed his way out of the room. His buddy—who, upon closer examination, looked like Ichabod Crane's uglier cousin—kept his spot beside Jessa, the knife still at her throat, and eyed her the way Ted Bundy did all of his victims. If I got my hands on him, I planned on whooping his ass the way his deddy should have, but for now, the pistol made me think better of it.

The gunman did a backward two-step down the hallway until we reached the living room, where the lamplight provided me a better look at him. He wore a half-zipped black hoodie, showing off a prison-inked chest, the word WHITE DEVIL tattooed across it in Old English. His gun hand bobbed around enough for me to see SS Bolts marked on the back of it, and he'd got a Swastika drawn on the other. Satanic symbols wound their way up his arms and twisted around his neck the way kudzu vines strangle tree trunks, and an upside-down cross took up most of the real estate on his forehead with the letters GFD through the middle of it. I didn't know what they stood for, but my first guess was goofy fucking dick.

He saw me sizing him up and made a show of doing the same. I didn't have no clothes on, and when his eyes glanced over my pecker, I said, "Your mama looked at it like that too."

His glazed eyes met mine, searching for some meaning he couldn't place a finger on. He asked, "Do what?"

"Your mama gets a real fond look in her eyes when she's got a hard pecker in her face," I said, scratching my ballsack, still tight from the threat made to Jessa.

"The hell you say?"

"I don't know, man." I shrugged. "You eyeing my pecker in such a way reminds me of some good times I shared with your mama."

"Hey, motherfucker, I ain't no faggot." He jabbed the pistol at me, adding emphasis to his words. "I ain't never sucked dick once in my life."

"Only cause you ain't never tried it," I said, scratching my ass in case I got the opportunity to hit him with a whiff of my own stink finger.

"What the fuck're we even talking 'bout?"

"How I might be your deddy."

"Yer starting to piss me off."

"Piss you off?" I asked. "Who woke who in the middle of the goddamn night?"

"Watch how you talk to me, boy."

I got serious now. "Call me boy again."

We stood in the middle of my living room—a violent strain stressing the silence between us. The gunman shifted his weight from foot to foot, the corner of his mouth twitching while he watched me, his arm shaky from aiming the pistol at me. I kept my arms at my sides and held back any insults I thought of now. I'd already done enough damage to his ego and didn't want to get my ass shot. He finally ended our standoff when he asked, "Where's yer brother?"

It was my turn to get confused, and I asked, "Do what now?"

"Do you know what these letters stand for?" He pointed at his forehead.

"That ain't what you asked me."

"I know it ain't. I'm asking you a new question."

"I'm sorry, I never learned how to interpret dumbass."

"One more of those, and yer getting a bullet between

the eyes, all right? Now . . . let me go ahead and tell you," he said, pulling his hood back, exposing his shaved head to the living room light. "Yer brother's done got himself into some shit with the Ghostface Devils. We're looking to settle up with him, and if you don't tell us where he's at, it's gonna get real bad for you."

I shriveled after hearing him ask for my little brother. "I don't know who the hell yall are, but I ain't talked to my brother for over a year. Now go on and get your ass outta my house."

"You ain't the one making demands here, boy."

"What'd I tell you 'bout calling me boy?" My fists clenched, and my toes dug into the shaggy carpet.

"What're you gonna do with a gun in your face?" The Ghostface Devil waved his firearm about like a magician coaxing a spell from the ether.

I lifted my hands, signaling to him nothing would happen right now, and said, "Lucky for you, I'm patient."

"Quit talking shit and tell me where your brother is."

"I already told you I don't know."

He went silent. His shooting eye lined me up with the sight, and his arm shook from holding the gun at arm's length for too long. The corner of his mouth curled back into a sneer, exposing a chipped canine tooth, and he started squinting to hold me in place. His index finger tapped at the trigger guard, not itching bad enough for him to give it a scratch, and he finally dropped his aim. The gunman stepped backward, reaching behind him for my living room door, and whistled. Ichabod appeared from my bedroom and made a wide berth around me.

Before leaving, the gunman said, "I'm gonna make you a deal. We'll give you a few days to find out where your brother is, and if you ain't figured it out by the time we come back, we're gonna make that pretty lady of yours watch what happens when our words ain't obeyed."

3.

When I got back in bed, sleep avoided me until sunlight peeped through the bedroom curtains, and I finally drifted off into unconsciousness. Andy waited for me on the other side of my eyelids, but Randy Jessup didn't accompany her in this dream. The Ghostface Devil escorted her into the spotlight of my mind's eye, a gun held to her head, slurring vile and violent threats about how he'd like to violate her. I hacked at the curtains of my imaginings, trying to rouse my consciousness, but I couldn't wake myself up.

I jerked awake when a weight thumped onto my chest and found Jessa standing over me. She'd already gotten ready for work, her makeup done, and her hair curled the way she knew I liked, but she wore a scowl on her face that didn't enhance her beauty. It said I broke her trust somehow, and I couldn't figure out what I did until I looked down and saw the bottle of Woodford lying next to me.

Jessa's fists punched into her hips, and she said, "How you feeling this morning, sweetness? Need some Aspirin for a headache or anything?"

"I ain't hungover." It's the only thing I could think to say, and it was the wrong answer.

"How much drinking did you do last night?"

"I didn't do any drinking last night."

"I remember you getting outta bed, Mack. You didn't come back for a while."

I raised onto my elbows, sitting up straight. If Jessa wasn't aware of our visitors last night, I wanted to keep it that way, but I couldn't think of an appropriate lie. I could say I got out of bed to have a drink, but I was already tiptoeing through a minefield because of it. She might leave me if I said it's what I did.

"I got outta bed—"

"Don't lie to me," she said, her eyes glimmering from tears or anger or both. "I'll walk out that door right now if you lie to me. I won't come back either."

"Jessa, I was drinking before you got home last night. I hid that bottle behind the geraniums when I saw you pull in. I didn't get outta bed to keep drinking, all right? I went and laid on the couch."

"Why'd you go lay on the couch?

"Cause I was having them dreams again, and I didn't wanna wake you up." It's the truest lie I could think of, and Jessa's face softened when she heard it.

"Why don't you go talk to somebody about 'em?"

"There ain't nobody to talk to in Tugalo County."

Jessa sat on the bed next to me and tickled my beard with her fingernails. "You could go to Athens or Atlanta or somewhere like that."

"How we gone afford it?"

"We'll figure it out somehow." Her voice hitched, and I took her hand, kissing each of her knuckles.

We sat that way until Jessa let out a forlorn sigh and said, "I gotta finish getting ready for work."

She stood up, and I shoved the blankets aside. "I gotta

go get ready too. It's gone be a late one for me. It's the last day of practice."

"You want me to reheat them steaks, and we can have 'em when you get home tonight?"

"Sounds good. Want me to pick anything up 'fore I come home?"

"I don't think so," she said, leaving the bedroom. "If I think of anything, I'll stop by the dollar store and get it."

"All right," I said, opening the closet and getting my clothes out to coach in. I didn't tell her about a visit I planned on making on my way to the high school.

4.

When I rolled up to the chain-link gate that kept people from driving onto Peanut's compound, a dog-faced motherfucker with a fat roll instead of a chin got out of a pickup with an AR slung over his shoulder. He wore overalls with a walkie-talkie clipped on the front and looked down at me over a pair of Ray-Bans. I recognized him from high school. Brent Ford didn't have no friends because he liked fighting too much and didn't care who ran in his circle. Not much changed with him living under his own roof. Now he only hurt who Peanut told him to.

Brent leaned into the window of my pickup, filling the interior with a smoky funk. I assumed he still smoked a couple of packs of Winston Reds a day, and when he opened his mouth to speak, I missed what he said because I couldn't keep my eyes from looking at his peanut-colored teeth.

"What'd you say?" I asked.

"I said you need to go on and back on outta here cause Peanut ain't seeing nobody today. He ain't in no mood for the company."

"I ain't here to keep him company. We got some business to talk over."

"Whatever business you got to talk about can be done on a different day. Back your truck up and get on outta here."

I wasn't in no mood to get ordered around like some know nothing peckerwood and let Brent hear it. "You need to open up that gate right there 'fore I get outta this truck and whoop your ass. I never got the chance in high school and wouldn't mind making up for lost time."

"You got a big mouth for being nothing but a pussy," Brent said, ripping off his sunglasses and letting me see his bloodshot eyes. "If I remember correctly, you wasn't doing no ass whooping in school. You was too busy munching out the bunghole of that dead girl."

"I ain't fixing to tell you again, Brent. Get that gate open, or I'll make sure you walk with a limp for the rest of your life."

Brent smacked the roof of my truck, said, "You know what, you done pissed me off now. Get outta there, and I'll show you what a real ass whooping looks like, boy."

"What'd you call me?"

"Goddamn, how many times am I gonna have to repeat myself with you, huh?" Brent backed away from my truck, shrugging the AR's sling over his head. "Not only are you a pussy, but you're stupid too. Can't hear a word I say."

Growing up, Deddy always said, men with a size advantage would underestimate my capacity for meanness, and since there wasn't no such thing as a fair fight, I ought to use it against them.

I sat in my truck, waiting for Brent to turn his back and lean the rifle against the fence, and when he took his eyes off me, I reached into the side pocket of my door and grabbed a tire knocker—a solid piece of hickory with a hitch ball crowning the end.

Before Brent turned back to me, I flung my door open, called out his name, and when he started to pivot, I swung the tire knocker at his kneecap like Hammerin' Hank swinging at a baseball. The sound his knee made when it imploded reminded me of a tree branch snapping, and the holler he let out made my turd hole pucker.

Brent floundered in the dirt, clutching his knee and cussed every member of my family tree, and I struck his knee a second time, crushing his fingers and turning his whole leg into taffy.

If he ever walked naturally again, it'd take a miracle from God, and I figured God liked Brent less than I did.

I unclipped the radio from the front of his overalls, snapped it onto my belt, and said, "You lay right there, you fat sumbitch, unless you want me feeding you this fucking thing, you understand?"

Brent couldn't do nothing but sob, and I walked over to the fence, flung his AR into the woods, and rolled the gate open wide enough for me to drive my pickup through. After I got back behind the wheel, I keyed the walkie and said, "Peanut, if you got your ears on, you need to get an ambulance out here for your boy. He's having some knee problems."

Peanut's voice replaced the static after I ended my transmission and said, "What the fuck you done did, Mack?"

"I did you a favor." I held the walkie out the window and keyed it, filling the other end with Brent's crying.

"Goddammit! The only favors I want from you are the ones I ask for."

"You'll thank me for this one later."

"I ain't in the mood for yer bullshit today." Peanut

hollered so loud I almost heard him from his front porch. "What the fuck do you want?"

"Me and you need to have a talk."

"If I thought we needed to have a talk, I would've called you."

"Well, I'm calling you."

Peanut didn't respond, and I sat in my truck listening to the radio fizzle.

When the silence didn't get broken, I said, "Peanut, I'm coming up there, and I ain't in the mood to get shot at. After I say my piece, I'll get outta your hair."

"Whatever you got to say," Peanut said through the static, "make it quick."

I tossed the walkie-talkie onto the passenger's seat and drove through the gate.

5.

Peanut waited on his front porch, leaning against the banister, resting his arms one on top of the other, staring down at me with a baleful eye. His front lip poked out from a large pinch of dip, and he spat in the dirt when I parked my truck.

Men were lined across his front porch with ARs aimed at the dirt or the sky, forming a wall to keep me from getting too close. I never knew the Bohannons to have this much security on hand. In Tugalo County, they were one step away from godhood, and nobody wanted to hurt them. Anyone who ended up having threatening thoughts toward the family knew they would have to deal with Caudell and would soon forget any violence they dreamed up, but I didn't see Caudell around.

I got out of my truck and brought the tire knocker with me. It wouldn't do nothing to stop a bullet, but it made Peanut's henchmen flinch when I got close enough, which is what I wanted. If they thought I was crazy enough to bring a wooden thumper to a gunfight, they might hesitate to squeeze the trigger, or it might just make them get itchy quicker, but I knew no bullets would get fired without Peanut's say-so first.

I watched Peanut's irritation with me diminish and replace with good humor. A smile crept across his face, and his cheeks got rosy the further it stretched. A hardy chuckle developed in his chest, and soon enough, his shoulders bounced from laughing so hard. Unsure of how to react, his men diverted their eyes from me, watching birds fly over, gazed off into the woods, or concentrated on the blinking towers of Albermarle Mountain.

After Peanut composed himself, he swiped a hairy forearm across his eyes and spat a streak of brown juice into Katie's azaleas. He stood up to his full height, shoved his hands into his pockets, and let his rough baritone fill the air. "What you know good now, Mack?" He let the question linger for a wink and said, "What's got you barging onto my property like you're Buford-damn-Pusser?"

I knocked the ball hitch against my bootheels the way some sluggers did before stepping into the batter's box. All eyes fell to the weapon in my hand, and I watched Peanut's lackeys get nervous. They shifted their weight back and forth, their eyeballs twitched in their sockets, and they adjusted their grips on their rifles. Peanut rolled his eyes at my display and went back to leaning on the porch railing.

"You quit intimidating the boys anytime you want." Peanut spat. "They ain't Caudell. That's for damn sure."

"Why don't I see Caudell nowhere?" I asked.

"Caudell's on vacation."

"Hopefully somewhere tropical."

"You know how much Caudell likes the beach."

"You send my brother on vacation with him?"

Peanut's ears perked at the question like a dog hearing a sound its master couldn't. "Naw, Marshall ain't on vacation with Caudell, but he's safe. If that's what you're wondering."

"It's not," I said and lifted the tire knocker to rest on my shoulder. "But I would like to know what kinda shit you've got Marshall into."

Peanut scratched his beard with a set of grimy finger-nails and eyed me through squinted lids. "How long's yer brother been working for me now?" He asked. "'More than a year now, right? In all that time, you ain't never once come by here wondering how he's doing or what kinda trouble I got him into. Far as I know, you two ain't talked to each other in all that time. What's got you curious about him now, Mack?"

"It's some personal business, Peanut."

Peanut's smile flattened, and he spat into the yard. "You oughta know that Marshall's business is my business."

"Don't fuck around with me today." I aimed the ball hitch between his eyes. "I'm in a damn bad mood."

"If I'm not mistaken, yer who's fucking with me." He put a chokehold on the banister, the wood creaking under his hands. "What kinda condition am I gone find Brent Ford in? More importantly, how much are his doctor bills gone cost me?"

"He might need a new knee."

"You bust his leg with that damn stick right there?"

"He's lucky I didn't crack his fucking jaw."

"I swear, every time you come around, I'm replacing somebody around here. Yall boys hear that? Try and mess with Mack, and you'll be looking for new employment." Peanut smiled at me. "What Brent ought to have done is shoot you on sight. He's always done his thinking with his fists. You probably got him raring for a fight. Ain't always smart having somebody like him around."

"Where you hiding my brother at, Peanut?"

"Don't worry about it, Mack. Marshall's okay."

"I ain't worried about his well-being. I'm here about mine."

Peanut dropped his elbows onto the banister and leaned all his weight onto them. He spat again and said, "What's got you worrying about yer well-being? Can't be because of Jessa's deddy. Last time I saw him, he was limping around because she shot him in the fucking foot. Funny as hell seeing that man act all pitiful."

"This visit ain't about Jessa's deddy."

"Then let's quit tangoing, Mack, and you tell me what's going on."

"Why do I got some Ghostface Devils breaking into my house while I'm sleeping wanting to know where the hell Marshall is?"

Peanut turned his face into a shoulder, hiding the shock twisting up his features, but when he spoke, he couldn't hide the alarm spiking his tone. "Do what now?"

"I ain't repeating myself."

"When did this happen?" He stared down at me now, his eyes violent orbs bugging out of their sockets.

"Last night."

"Why ain't you called me already?"

"I'm here right now, ain't I?"

"They ain't a group you wanna fuck with, Mack," Peanut growled more than spoke, and a nervosity spread among his henchmen so that they began trading fearful glances they hoped the boss man didn't see. "Get somewhere out of the way and let me worry about 'em."

"Why am I getting caught up in your bullshit, Peanut?"

"Watch that tone with me."

"They came into my house and held a knife to my girlfriend's throat. You'll get whatever tone I give you." I strode forward until I almost stood under Peanut's nose. "Now tell me why I'm getting caught up in your bullshit?"

Peanut pointed a finger at me. "Take a minute and think about all the bullshit I've shoveled for you and then correct yer tone."

"What did you have my brother do, Peanut?"

"What I asked him to."

I bashed the ball hitch against the bottom step of Peanut's front porch and made his men fidget all around. "Be straight with me."

"This's as straight as it's gone get."

"They held a knife to Jessa's throat."

Peanut sighed. "Listen to me, Mack. Get yer girlfriend and take a break. These boys ain't like that preacher. They're some bloodthirsty sumbitches and ain't gone toy around with you. Yer gone wake up one morning, and yer brain's gone be scrambled eggs, but before they let you die, they'll make sure you get to watch how many different ways they know how to hurt Jessa. I'm telling you not to put her at risk. Get outta Tugalo County 'til I say it's safe to come home, hear me?"

"Tell my brother I'm looking for him," I said, heading back to my truck.

Peanut waited until I yanked myself in behind the wheel and hollered, "Hey, Mack, how's them Titans looking."

"Like a football team," I answered.

He laughed, said, "Let Coach Cole know us boosters got a check in the mail for him."

6.

I first saw Montgomery Alan Cole throw during a junior high football game, playing for the Blackwood County Cubs. He stood half a foot taller than all the boys on either team, and when he slung the pigskin, it streaked over the field like a bolt of lightning. He could also outrun any pursuing defender, and when we hit him, it was like running into one of those concrete barriers drunk drivers wrap their cars around.

Now, I'm the kind of sore loser who changes the rules mid-game or just quits playing altogether, but there was something about how Monty played where losing didn't hurt so much. Each time he lined up under center, it was like witnessing an artist pick up a brush and step in front of a canvas. It left everyone in awe with how he diagnosed the defense and directed his receivers through traffic. Monty's coach just let him go out and play because he took control of the game, and there was no scripting some of what he did.

Blackwood whooped Tugalo County on the night I remember, and it was the first of many losses I'd suffer to a team Monty played for. We got to be good friends, though. I went to him after a high school game one Friday evening and told him we should hit a fishing pond I knew of; he brought the beers and the girls, and even after becoming a highly recruited SEC prospect, we still snuck off to that pond.

Monty blew out his knee during spring practice one year, and after the doctor looked at his X-ray, he said the inside of his leg looked like the wreckage of Hiroshima. Despite hard work and rehab, there was no nursing his knee back to its previous condition, and Monty never threw the ball the same again. It didn't have the same zip, and Monty tried to force throws once too often. The coaches put him on the bench with a clipboard, and that's how he discovered his love for coaching.

After Monty got the head job for the Tugalo County Titans, he called me up one morning and asked if I'd like a spot on his staff. I no-showed my job back then, and the high school put me on the payroll. Officially, I'm listed as a janitor, but I don't never clean no toilets or nothing unless Jessa tells me to do it at home. Small town schools have to get creative with staffing in the athletic department.

When I walked into the locker room, one of the kids told me Coach Cole was waiting for me in his office. I knocked on the door before opening it. Monty called me in, and I found him kicked back in his chair with his feet propped on his desktop. Next to his sneakers were dust-covered trophies he'd won during his high school career.

He replayed a video from practice the day before, watching who we thought could be our starting quarterback throw against the first-string defense. I watched Monty rewind the tape after a defensive back intercepted the ball. The offense lined up in the shotgun with three wide receivers spread out wide; a running back went into motion and filled the slot. A linebacker teased a blitz, but when he dropped back into coverage, the quarterback got confused, forcing an interception. Monty watched the play again before speaking to me.

"Go on and have a seat, Mack." Monty peered at me from underneath the bill of his blue and silver ball cap with a T stitched in the center.

After I sat, he started playing the tape again and said, "Watch him. He don't even try to go through his progressions. Just throws deep. Thinks because he's got a rocket-fucking-arm, he'll just outthrow the defense. That gunslinger shit's gone get us beat."

"It's July, Monty, you got time to break him of it."

Monty dropped his feet on the floor, leaned across his desk, and rested his chin on the remote control. "It's what I'm trying to do, but the season starts in about a month, and the kid don't wanna listen." He watched the TV over my shoulder. "I think I might drop him to second string and see what it does to his head."

I shrugged. "You know more about quarterbacks than I do. It's why you got them trophies right there."

"Yeah, that don't mean shit when you're coaching. Especially when his deddy gets to talking to him and that numbnuts private instructor they hired thinks he knows more than I do. Let that little bastard try coaching this team. He ain't never won shit."

"You've dealt with all this before," I said, turning to rewatch the play. I couldn't tell if the QB could get full blame for the interception or if the defensive back made an outstanding play. From an athletic perspective, the DB was every coach's wet dream—tall, long arms and ran faster than a cheetah fixing to kill its supper. If our coaching staff could get him noticed, he'd play for a powerhouse college on the D1 level.

"How you think the linebackers looked yesterday?"

I slung an arm over the back of my chair, said, "They did all right. Didn't have to holler at 'em as much as I did the day before. Problem is, they ain't got no better at setting the edge, and if you wasn't such a pass-happy sumbitch, yall'd run it right down our throat."

Monty crossed his arms and eyeballed me. "I'm thinking of moving Franklin to the offense. His ball skills make him a goddamn nightmare."

"Why don't you rewind that tape?" I said, fingering the TV. "Ain't nobody else gone make a play for the ball like that."

"I know it. The kid'll put up video game numbers at wide receiver."

"I don't know if I'd go that far."

"You're full of shit, and you know it."

"I ain't trying to lose my best defensive back, Monty."

Monty aimed the remote at the TV and turned it off. He opened a drawer on his left-hand side and dropped the remote in it with a clatter. "I ain't for sure what I'm gone do yet, but it's probably gone happen."

"All right," I said, leaning back, "if you move Franklin to offense, then I want Mosley on defense."

"Hell no, you're asking for my best offensive lineman."

"You know he'd be hell at defensive end. Kid's mean as shit."

"Ain't happening, but listen," Monty said, pushing himself up in his chair and dropping his eyes to the desktop. "You look like shit today, Mack. You looked like shit the day before and the day before that. How much you been drinking here lately?"

"Enough to get me buzzed, but no more than that. I told you I'd cut back on how much I'm drinking."

"You know I can't be your babysitter," Monty stabbed a finger at the locker room. "I already got a whole team full of teenagers, and I need you to be responsible for yourself."

"Where the hell's this coming from? Jessa call you up or something?"

Monty joggled his leg with such force his trophies danced a shaky jig, and the TV rattled from all the vibrating.

"She did call you up, didn't she?"

"Mack, it don't make a damn if she called me or not. I been planning on having this conversation with you regardless. Some boosters have said they smell whiskey on your breath."

"Those're the same assholes who get me liquored up."

"Maybe they do, but they ain't the ones who're getting talked about."

"Who's talking 'bout me?"

"It don't make a damn who's talking 'bout you. I'm telling you to get your drinking under control. If anybody who means a damn starts talking, it'll cause me trouble. Worse than that, if it affects your coaching ability, I'll have to make a decision I don't want to."

"Listen, Monty," I said, leaning forward, propping my elbows on my knees. "I've only been drinking enough to help me get to sleep. Them dreams I been having keep me up all hours of the night. It's why I look like I been hit by a truck every day when I get here."

Monty looked at me for the first time since this conversation started—his eyes flickered the way they did whenever the offense broke a big play or when they turned the ball over on a fumble or an interception, disguising just how angry he might be.

"Mack, you're one of my best friends in the whole damn

world. Been that way since we was kids. It's why I brought you onto my staff. You got a great football mind, and the kids fucking love you. I don't wanna hear no excuses about why you're drinking." He paused and glared at me until I broke his stare, looking down at my clenched fists. "If you can't get no sleep at night, then go to a doctor who can help you. I done told you the guidance counselor here can set you up with somebody. Won't nobody but me and you ever know about it, all right?"

"I hear you."

"Do you hear me?"

I looked up, locking my eyes onto Monty's, and nodded hard.

"I didn't wanna have this conversation no more than you did, but I worry 'bout you."

"You ain't got to."

"Well, I do." He placed his hands on his desk, pushed himself out of his chair, and stood over me. "Don't go and say nothing to Jessa about this. She ain't said word one to me."

"She's said plenty to me about it."

"Only cause she loves you, Mack. I can't remember you ever sticking with a girl this long."

"Mama says the same."

"Maybe that oughta tell you something." Monty stepped around his desk and slapped me on the shoulder on his way out of the office.

7.

Conroy lifted a foot, signaling Franklin into motion, and called a combination of numbers and colors. An outside linebacker crept up toward the line of scrimmage, disguising from where the blitz would come. A quiet murmur fell over the field, and an electric anticipation buzzed through the players.

Conroy dropped back three steps after the ball got snapped, but before he could plant his feet and throw, a defensive end smashed through his left tackle, knocking him on his ass. Conroy side-stepped the linemen and evaded getting plowed over but couldn't step up into the pocket for a linebacker getting in his face. He scrambled and booked it for the sideline, the linebacker only getting his fingertips on Conroy's jersey.

He kept his eyes downfield, fooling everyone where he would go with the ball, and flung it across his body. It bulleted over to Franklin and hit him right in the numbers. The boy ran with bad intentions, lighting up a defensive back who came at him too high, putting his shoulder pads right in the kid's chest and running him over. Franklin spun and danced and hopped, dodging and jigging his way out of tackles, and sprinted down the sideline once he got free. His teammates escorted him downfield and celebrated after he crossed the goal line.

Monty blew his whistle, ending the offense's celebration, and threw his hat in the grass. "Goddamn, Connie, helluva play there, son. Why ain't you got that awareness all the time?"

"He ain't been having me to look for, Coach," Franklin said, spiking the ball on the field.

"The hell I need you for?" Conroy asked. "You won't be open every time."

"The hell I won't."

"Go eat a dick, Franky."

"Dick don't taste as good as your mama." Franklin grinned from behind his face mask.

Conroy spun on a heel and punched Franklin's shoulder pads. "The fuck did you just say?"

Monty blew his whistle, trying to mute Franklin's comeback, but Franklin only spoke louder. "Your mama be letting me get taste tests, Connie. She got a different flavor for me every night."

"Franklin," I hollered and marched toward the middle of the field where the boys were. "Shut your ass up and go get hydrated."

"Hey, Coach Dooley." Franklin lifted his hands like he meant no harm. "I'm just having fun."

"Well, you're having fun at the wrong fucking position. Now Coach is gone move you to offense."

"I kinda like playing on offense," he said, jogging toward the Powerade cooler.

Monty met me at the fifty, said, "He did look damn good out there, didn't he?"

"That was one play, and nobody tried covering him. It don't make the kid Hines-fucking-Ward."

Monty reached for his sunglasses, yanking them off. His eyes pulsed in their sockets, and I turned, following his stare toward the visitor's stands. Ichabod leaned over the railing, greasy strands of hair covering the upside-down cross inked in the middle of his forehead. He stared back at me, reminding me of the knife he held to Jessa's throat, and my pecker shriveled from the violent considerations filling my mind.

"Who the hell is that?" Monty asked.

"I ain't never seen him before," I answered, my voice raw in my throat.

"Well, he needs to get his ass off our field."

"I'll go talk to him."

I strode toward the stands where the Ghostface Devil waited for me. He wore a black tank top, showing off the tattoos covering his arms and chest. Hate symbols decorated most of his body, but he also wore quotes in languages I couldn't read. The man stood tall when I got close and raked the blade of his knife along the railing. My ears perked from the scraping sound, and he gave me a snaggle-tooth smile. "That's a real fast nigger y'all got there."

"Say it again and see if I don't come up there and whoop your ass."

He smiled wider and said, "A white man ought not to get so defensive over an inferior race."

"Get your ass outta them stands and fuck off."

"Can't stop thinking about that pretty lady of yours." Ichabod's smile stretched so wide now it looked as though his face would tear. "Hope I get to see her again some-time soon."

My body got cold hearing him reference Jessa, and I turned. Monty stood at the opposite sideline with his hands on his hips, squinting into the sunshine.

"Don't you worry about him," Ichabod said. "Pay attention to me right now. You need to hear what I gotta say." He paused, waiting for me to turn back to him. When I did, he went on, "We're giving you 'til the weekend to find your brother. If you ain't found him by the time it's over, our next visit ain't gonna be a courtesy call."

"Meet me out in the parking lot, and we'll find out how bad you wanna see me again," I spoke through gritted teeth with flecks of spit torpedoing from the corners of my mouth.

"Don't go and get yourself riled up there, buddy. Hate for you to have to explain to the coach what I'm doing here. Already gonna be awkward enough, ain't it?"

I pointed a finger in his face. "Get your ass off this field before I kick it off."

He stared at me through razor slits, and his smile turned malevolent. "First part of you I'm gonna cut off is gonna be that finger right there. I'll let you watch me tickle your girlfriend with it."

It took all my energy not to leap into the stands and tear a new shithole into him. With Monty watching me, I needed to be careful about what I did. The last thing I wanted to do was get him in a position where he'd have to fire me.

Ichabod laughed, watching me struggle with my savage urges. He said, "Boy, you look like a dog who can't get off his leash to take a bite outta the mailman's ass."

"I'm gone tell you this one more time," I spoke low, my voice barely a whisper. "Get your ass off this field. We're having football practice."

I turned, leaving the Ghostface Devil behind, but before I could get out of earshot, he said, "Enjoy your weekend."

8.

After my confrontation with the Ghostface Devil, we ran the kids through a few situational drills, then broke practice for the remainder of the summer. Monty got them all to take a knee, told them to have a safe vacation, and we'd see them again in the fall. Once they headed for the locker room, I jogged to the parking lot, not wanting to get into it with Monty about who our visitor was. He didn't notice me leaving, so I got out of there without having to make up some excuse.

I got in behind the wheel of my truck and steered it for the horizon. The Blue Ridge Mountains were a jagged silhouette against the marmalade-colored sky—the curve of the sun still peeking over the chestnuts, attempting to keep its grasp upon the lingering moments of the day. The humidity created a heavy layer inside the cab of my truck despite the air conditioner blowing at full blast. My skin stung from sunburn and my temples throbbed from my encounter.

I drove in the opposite direction of home and headed into town. Abandoned warehouses marked my drive like weathered tombstones—their inscriptions too faded to display the date of passing. When I got to the Tugalo

County Credit Union, I took a detour through its parking lot to avoid stopping at a red light. It allowed me to skip traffic, and I flipped on my blinker at a four-way stop. A tow truck driver motioned me to take the right of way, and I steered onto Toccoa Street.

I parked behind a worn-out SUV and walked across a yard in need of raking, dry leaves crunching under my heels with every step. The front door stood open, and I tapped on the screen, announcing my presence. Some new reality show played on the TV, and a teacup-sized dog yipped at me from the couch. I heard footsteps approaching, stepped away from the screen, and waited in the grass.

Brystal Early's trim figure filled the screen, her kinky hair piled in a bun on top of her head, her eyes sunken from hardly sleeping. She got long-faced seeing me there and opened the door without a greeting. I stepped into the home, and her dog sniffed around my ankles. Brystal led me to the back porch, leaving the TV on for noise, and picked up the dog before stepping outside. We sat down at a patio table stained from grimy weather and didn't speak.

A lawnmower munched grass next door, and tires hummed over the road out front. The dog's eyes bugged out of its head while trying to keep up with all the sights going on around it. I studied Brystal from the corner of my eyes. Despite her sleepy countenance, she still looked pretty. Her angular features accentuated her cat-like eyes, and her plain face made her look girlish. My brother dated her casually, always waiting for the next best thing to come along, but Brystal latched onto Marshall like someone unwilling to give up on a slot machine, always believing she'd hit the jackpot.

Our silence finally got broken when Brystal shushed

the dog from barking at a bird and said, "I've been waiting for you to come by."

"You could've called me instead."

"I didn't wanna do that."

"How come?"

"Because I don't wanna talk about your brother."

I scratched the back of my head like it might get my thoughts stirring or provide me with the proper thing to say, but I barreled ahead. "What's Marshall got himself into, Brystal?"

Brystal let her dog down, sat back in her chair, and crossed one leg over the other. Her bottom lip curled into her mouth, and she nibbled on it like the pain would keep her from having to speak. She sighed, then said, "You really need to talk to your brother about what's going on with him."

"I wouldn't even be bothering you if I knew where he was hiding out at." I paused, hoping she'd fill in the blank. When she didn't, I said, "You know where he's been at?"

"He spent the night here a couple of days ago and was gone before I woke up. I ain't talked to him since."

"How'd he act when he was here?"

She looked over, a wistfulness filling her eyes. "Like we were the only two people alive."

"Marshall tell you anything I oughta know?"

Brystal shook her head.

"What ain't you telling me?"

"I really wish you wasn't here."

"I wouldn't be if I didn't need to know where Marshall was." Her dog sniffed at my ankles again. "You tell me where that is, and I'll leave you be."

"I don't know where your brother is, Mack."

"You get a visit from the Ghostface Devils?"

When Brystal looked over this time, her discontented longings were gone and got replaced by a touch of fear. "Why are you asking me about them?"

"Because they broke into my house and aimed a gun at me."

"Do whatever they ask you, Mack."

I leaned across the table, staring Brystal down. "They want me to tell 'em where Marshall is."

Brystal turned her head away.

"Who are these boys, Brystal?"

"Just tell them whatever you can to get them to leave you alone."

"Who are they?" My voice got hard.

"A gang of white supremacists you don't want nothing to do with."

"Why're they looking for Marshall?"

"Because they want to hurt him."

"What did my brother do?"

"I want you to leave now, Mack."

"What did he do, Brystal?"

Brystal got up from the patio table, clicking her tongue at her dog. When she picked it up off the ground, she looked at me and said, "Don't come back to my house again."

9.

fter returning to my truck, I sat behind the wheel, unable to catch my breath. My throat seized up, making it no bigger than a needle eye, and getting air into my lungs was more grueling than shoving a camel through. The shakes got ahold of me, and I grasped the steering wheel with a knuckle-white grip, muscles in my forearms stretched tight like rubber bands do right before they snap. A cold rush started behind my eyes and surged down to my toes, turning my shakes into shivers. It made my teeth chatter, and I cranked on the truck's heater to get them to go away.

Seeing Brystal gave life to dead memories, and they stumbled out of crypts that I entombed them in like zombies do in horror movies. Andrea led the preacher in these hallucinations, her pretty eyes pale and lifeless and her body gaunt and bruised. Randy Jessup stared at me with a single eyeball in the middle of his forehead, reading my thoughts and fears and exposing me to them all. He opened his mouth to preach, and his voice came forth like a bullhorn, drowning out all noise and sound, and I plugged my ears.

Brystal stood at her screen door, the dog cradled under

an arm, and watched me. I yanked the gear shift into reverse and let the truck's weight pull it backward. Letting her see me this way made my stomach clench, and I covered my mouth with a hand to keep from gagging. Once I got back onto the road, I shifted into drive and headed for the closest package store. I needed a drink and needed it before I went home to Jessa.

I turned off the heater when I got back to the four-way stop, my windows fogged up from the raised temperature, and I rolled them down to let cooler air in. The humidity replaced the hot air blowing out of my vents and sweat dripped from the tip of my nose. I turned the A/C dial until it could turn no further, and cold air blasted in my face. My shivers returned but not from the cold. I needed to get alcohol in my system to even out my nerves.

When I got to Fern's Package Store, only a few cars were parked in the spaces up front. I didn't recognize any license plates and figured I could get out of there without having to visit with anyone. Wearing my Titans' gear inside would make me stand out like a whore in church— people would want to speak with me and find out how the team looked. I didn't mind those sorts of conversations when I wasn't in a full-blown alcohol frenzy and trying to keep my drinking a secret.

A doorbell buzzed when I stepped inside. Nobody looked up from the labels they studied; only the guy behind the register bothered to acknowledge me. I beelined it for the bourbon aisle and picked out a bottle of Woodford. Before I approached the cash register, I pulled my ball cap low to keep my face from getting recognized and stared at the floor when I handed it to the cashier. He scanned the label and let me know my total. Before he bagged the bottle for me, he asked, "You're Coach Cole's assistant, ain't ya?"

I nodded, hoping he'd understand I needed to go.

"How's them Titans gone look this year? I hear good things 'bout that Conroy kid. Word is the little shit can sling it."

"He's got an arm, all right."

"Boy, I hope we go all the way this year," the cashier said, sliding my paper sack across the counter.

"We hope so too."

"Yall already got a game plan going for Blackwood?" The cashier counted out my change. "Them boys is always hell."

"We got some ideas." I tried stepping away from the counter.

"You know they can't handle the run. It's how McFalls County whooped 'em last year."

"McFalls County has got the running backs."

"You're damn right they do. Made Blackwood's defense look soft."

"Well, I'm gone get on outta here," I said, turning my back on the cashier.

"Hey, I'll letcha go."

Before I got out to my truck, I'd already torn the plastic wrap from around the cork and shoved the paper sack into a trash can outside. When the first drink hit my system, a warmth spread through me, setting my insides afire and calming my nerves while the flames spread. I breathed easier now, and my thoughts got to where I could control them, allowing me to shove Andrea back into a sepulcher of memories.

My cellphone buzzed in a cupholder, and I let it ring until it went to voicemail. After I took another swig of bourbon, I snatched it up and flipped it open to check my missed calls. Monty called while I'd been inside the store, and Jessa was who I let go to voicemail. I dialed the code that let me check my messages and waited for Jessa's voice to fill the speaker.

When it did, she asked, "Why am I getting a call from Coach Cole saying you stormed out after practice today? Something happen between yall two? He didn't sound like he was mad or nothing, but you probably need to call him. I hope ain't nothing wrong. Call me back. Love you."

I flipped the phone shut, setting it back in the cupholder, and drank until my chest burned. A purple hue colored the sky, and stars winked above me. My brain started getting foggy, and I knew I needed to get home before I was incapable of driving. I cranked the truck, and when I got back on the road, I decided to go see Mama before heading to the house.

10.

Mama lived in a single-wide right up the road from me and Jessa. She bought the property not too long after selling the house her and Deddy built together. It sat back up on a hill, surrounded by poplar trees and live oaks, with Albermarle Mountain providing background scenery. The radio towers at its peak blinked against a soot-colored sky, providing me the only light to navigate her gravel drive. I coasted underneath the carport next to her trailer and parked beside her new Ford pickup.

I reached under my seat for the bottle of Woodford, needing another drink to even me out. Tremors shook my body on the whole ride over, and I still thought with too much clarity. I didn't want to get to the point where my brain got so fuzzy I couldn't differentiate between the sober and the intoxified. What I did need to do, was get rid of the impressions Andy left on my thoughts after her most recent appearance. I couldn't have her influencing me while I tried to find out what Mama knew about Marshall.

After fishing the bottle from beneath my seat, I removed the cork and pulled hard. The familiar warmth spread through my chest, and I wiped my mouth with the back of my arm. I tossed the bottle onto the passenger's seat and opened the center console. I got a pack of chewing gum out and unwrapped a couple of sticks. Mama nagged me about my drinking habits more than Jessa did, saying I was going down the same road Deddy did before the Bohannons conned him into taking a fall and getting sent off to Sweetwater State Penitentiary. After I got the smell of whiskey off my breath, I sprayed myself with some cologne. I let the fragrance settle and then got out of the truck.

My steps were shifty at first, and I held onto my pickup for balance, letting my equilibrium reset. I closed my eyes to keep the world from spinning, figuring I wouldn't get dizzy if I couldn't see the world moving like a tilt-a-whirl. Once I got brave enough to open them again, I let go of my truck and put one foot in front of the other. The ground swayed underneath me, and I wondered if this was how toddlers perceived the world when they learned to walk. I reached out for Mama's truck and used it to sustain my footing. After my feet got moving again, I closed an eye to keep from seeing double and aimed myself at her front porch. If I could make it there, I could get inside the mobile home.

After completing my trek across Mama's front yard, I grabbed ahold of a porch rail and held onto it as if it kept me from spilling into some great chasm. My knees wobbled ascending the front porch steps, and it looked like I practiced some hillbilly two-step. Porch slats shifted underneath my bootheels but didn't trip me. I reached the screen door and leaned into it, breathing for the first time since beginning this journey.

I knocked on the front door to let Mama know I waited outside, but when she didn't come to answer it, I cupped my hands around my eyes and peered into its diamond-shaped window. There were no lights on in the living room, and the inside of the single-wide was shrouded in darkness. It was unlike Mama to leave no lights on, and I jiggled the door handle to see if she locked it. The door opened a crack, and I stepped through.

"Mama?"

My question got no answer, and the drunk I'd worked on since leaving Fern's Package Store dissipated there on the spot. The crown of my head started tingling and sweat pearled on my shoulders and back. My legs stiffened, and my instincts told me to head back to the truck for my thumper. Enough alcohol still circulated through me, so I didn't listen to them. Mama kept a hiking staff next to the front door, and I reached out for it, but it was gone.

"Mama, you home?"

I stepped deeper into the trailer and switched on a living room lamp. Soft lighting lit the trailer, and nothing seemed out of sorts. Mama left a stack of envelopes on the counter next to a Dave Robicheaux novel with the TV remote lying on top. I didn't see her purse anywhere but found her truck keys hanging on a kitchen hook. My body froze when I heard movement come from her bedroom, and I turned to see Marshall standing in the doorway.

My brother had grown his hair out since I saw him last, and a coarse beard covered his face. He gazed at me with hardscrabble eyes, his pupils cold and unnerving. A crude line set across his face, and he breathed in shallow breaths. His knuckles were busted and bloody, and he flexed his fingers into tight fists, tensing the muscles throughout his forearms and shoulders.

I took a fighting stance in case Marshall decided we needed to work out our issues. After he choked back a sob, my body went slack, and I reached for a wall. A weakness spread through me, and I thought my knees might give out, but I remained upright. I watched Marshall wrestle with his cries until he formed them into words.

Once he spoke, his voice came out in a chilling tone, and he said, "They got Mama, Coy."

PART TWO

ICHABOD'S CONFESSIONS

1.

Sobriety kicked my drunken state of being harder than a steel toe boot square in the nuts. Thoughts of Jessa's safety pierced my cerebrum like a fishing hook puncturing the skin. I spun on my brother, ignoring whatever else he started to say, and stumbled for the door, but my feet tripped over one another, and I crawled further than I walked. Marshall got to me and helped me heave myself off the floor, telling me I smelled like a bottle of whiskey, and I shoved him away. Without shutting it behind me, I burst out the front door and took a tumble down the porch steps. Marshall came outside, locked the door, then came to my aid, but I sat up before he reached me.

Marshall grabbed ahold of my arm without me reaching for him and yanked me to my feet.

"Don't fucking touch me," I said.

"How much you done drunk tonight, Coy? Your eyeballs is swimming all around your head."

"Mind your goddamn business."

He held up a hand, asked, "I ain't letting you get behind the wheel of that truck unless you can tell me how many fingers I'm holding up."

"Fuck off, Marshall."

"Be mad at me all you want," Marshall stepped around me, beating me to the driver's side door, "I'm just looking out for ya."

"You ain't driving my truck."

"You're too drunk to stop me."

"I ain't drunk."

"You can't even talk straight."

I charged my brother, but he'd always been quicker than me, especially after drinking my weight in bourbon. He caught me around my waist, wrestled me over the side of the truck, and dumped me in the bed. The truck's body shifted with the addition of my weight, and Marshall held his hands out to his sides to keep his balance. He planted a knee in the middle of my chest, pinning me to the truck bed, and slapped the sides of my jeans until he found which pocket I kept my keys in. Before I could stop him from taking them, Marshall confiscated the keys and hopped over the side.

He got in behind the wheel, cranked the truck, and I rolled out, landing with a hard thump in the gravel. Marshall opened the passenger's side door for me, and I used the door handle to get to my feet. He saw me eyeing the spot where I left my bottle of Woodford and said, "I tossed it out the window. If you'd rather have it than go wherever it is you're trying to get, then go crawl through the dirt for it like some wino."

"You're gone pay me back for that."

"The hell I am. You got your money's worth."

I snatched my cellphone from the cup holder and saw two more missed calls from Jessa after I flipped it open. She didn't bother leaving a voice mail either time, and I punched the redial button. I held the phone to my ear and listened to it ring until it went to voicemail. Marshall saw the worry in my eyes and left Mama's without asking where to go. I called Jessa a second time and counted out the rings until I got sent back to her voicemail. Stomach acid surged to the back of my throat, and I grabbed ahold of the dashboard, bracing myself for whatever might come up, but I hadn't eaten all day—and only dry heaved until my body racked with pain and tears blurred my vision.

"What the hell you done to yourself, Coy? I ain't never seen you get this way."

"Get me to my trailer, Marshall."

"Mama said you don't do nothing but sit around and drink no more. I can't imagine Jessa has anything different to say."

"You been gone too damn long to start lecturing me like this."

"How long I'm gone don't change the fact that I'm still your brother."

"Maybe you should've thought about that before you chose Peanut's business over me."

Marshall got quiet at my words and drove in silence until we reached my trailer. He sped across the yard, parking in front of the porch, allowing me to hop straight out of the truck and bound up the steps. Jessa met me at the front door, and I scooped her into my arms, squeezing her the way I would if she were some long lost love. She wiggled out of my embrace and said, "What's done got into you, Mackenzie? How much you done drunk tonight?"

"I ain't had that much to drink."

If Jessa heard me speak, she disregarded my defense. Her eyes went past me to where my brother stood, and her fingernails dug into my arms and pinched the skin, her breath caught in her throat, and she spoke at a volume only I could hear. "What's your brother doing here?"

"I got a lot I need to tell you." Another wave of sobriety spilled over me, and I knew Jessa needed to hear the truth.

2.

Jessa sat on the couch across from me, her eyes sparkling brighter than a July 4th fireworks display, barely able to contain her anger. Marshall reclined in a La-Z-Boy he hadn't sat in for over a year, and his eyes flittered like he might fall asleep. I waited for Jessa to light into me about what happened the night before, but she got up and started pacing the living room. She crossed her arms over her chest, stared at her toes dragging through the carpet, and clenched her jaw, so the muscles got taut.

"So you're telling me," the words barreled out of her like a freight train, "some men broke into our trailer last night, and one of 'em held you at gunpoint while the other held a knife to my throat?"

I nodded.

"And you didn't wake me up?"

"It wasn't one of them types of situations, Jessa."

"And they're looking for Marshall right there?" Jessa pointed at my brother.

"That's what they said."

"And now they got your mama to bring him outta hiding?"

"That's what we think."

Jessa stood in the middle of the living room now, her eyes weighing down on me until they got me feeling like a child about to get his tail whooped. "And what the hell do yall plan on doing about this?"

Marshall kicked the footrest down, sat up in his chair, and echoed Jessa's question. "What the hell do we plan on doing about this, Coy?"

"We gotta get Mama back."

"I know yall gotta get your mama back," Jessa said. "I wanna know how many of these bastards yall plan on hurting in the process? I don't goddamn appreciate having a knife held to my throat like I'm some farm animal meant for slaughter. I'll go get your deddy's gun from the safe right now and go shoot 'em up myself if I have to." Jessa stabbed a finger in my face. "Don't you even speak a word, Mack. If I say that's what I'm gonna do, then that's what I'm gonna do."

I held up my hands, knowing there was no sense in arguing with Jessa when she got in a frenzy like this. God forbid she get ahold of Deddy's guns—she put a bullet hole in her own deddy for doing less than this. "I ain't fixing to try and talk you outta shit, Jessa. We gotta find out where these boys is keeping Mama first. Once we do that, we can walk a mudhole through 'em."

A smile brightened Marshall's face, and he said, "It turns me on when you talk dirty like that, Coy."

"Don't act crude, Marshall," Jessa said, "not in front of me anyway."

"Shit, girl, your middle name is crude. I've heard the stories."

Jessa's eyes cut over at me.

"Not from me he didn't."

Marshall whooped. "Damn if Jessa Rae ain't got you pussy-whipped, son. Never thought I'd see the day."

"Shut the hell up," I murmured.

Marshall kicked the footrest back up and reclined until he stretched out in the chair, said, "Damn if it ain't good seeing you again, Coy. I been missing you."

"Where you been at anyway, Marshall?" Jessa asked. "You could've stopped by here anytime you wanted."

"I've been working my ass off for Peanut if you ain't heard. Me and Caudell was doing a job for him down in Atlanta. It's how we got tangled up with them peckerwood ass pubes."

I leaned forward, resting my forearms on my knees. "What's the story behind all that, Marshall? I went by Peanut's earlier today, and he's got half of Fort Benning watching over the place. Said you and Caudell were both on vacation."

"It's a long story, Coy, and I don't feel like telling it right now."

"The hell you say?" Jessa said. "It's cause of you a man broke into my house last night and put a knife to my throat. You'll sit here and tell every detail, even if we have to stay up half the night."

"I don't know if you know this or not, but it's my name that's on the lease. You're in my house."

I watched Jessa's face turn a hard shade of ruby-red. The last time it got that color, we were out drinking at the Due South, and some girl hit on me. After Jessa informed her of our relationship, the girl said until there was a ring on my finger, it made me fair game. Three bouncers did their best to pry Jessa off that girl while I sat by, sipping my beer. I could've offered those boys my assistance, but one thing I've learned is not to interfere with Jessa whenever she's ripping some girl a new cooter hole.

I got off the couch, took Jessa by the arm, and led her to our bedroom, getting her away from my brother before she opened a can of whoop-ass. I shut the door behind us, folded my arms around her, and held her until she relaxed. My brother could get people riled up in a way where they got familiar with violent aspects of human nature they'd never known before, and there were no exceptions to this.

Once Jessa got to breathing normally again, I held her out at arm's length and said, "You ain't gone like what I'm fixing to say, but I need you to listen to me, all right?"

I waited for her to nod her agreement and went on, "I don't know who or what kinda trouble me and Marshall are fixing to have to get into to get Mama back, but I can't be worrying about you getting hurt. I ain't saying you can't help or can't take care of yourself. I'm saying I can't focus on what needs to get done if you're in harm's way."

Silence flickered between us, and Jessa laid her head on my chest. She reached her arms around me and ran her fingernails over my back, leaving a trail of goosebumps behind. "Sweetness," she said, "if you need me to go into hiding to get your mama back, that's fine. But you better make damn sure to hurt the man who held a knife to my throat so bad his mama feels it."

3.

After Jessa packed a bag, we shoved ourselves into my truck with her sitting in the middle, resting a hand on my thigh. Marshall spun the dial on my radio until he found a classic rock station playing some CCR. John Fogerty sang about some trouble being on the way, and I wondered if this wasn't some divine message, letting us know of a long night that laid ahead. The thought got whisked away by Marshall's singing, and I added my voice to his, refusing to allow my fears to strangle me blind. Jessa joined in, sounding prettier than either of us, and when the song ended, we laughed together, and a kinship filled the truck—a feeling I'd become unfamiliar with and didn't want to lose.

Blue Oyster Cult blasted through the speakers after a commercial break ended, but none of us sang along. The crown of my head prickled from the gloomy lyrics, and I distracted myself by focusing on the road. It snaked through the Blue Ridge foothills, leading us deep into the country. The world got quiet out here, and I twisted the volume knob to hear it better. Marshall let his window down, and a gust of humid air blew his hair from his eyes. Albermarle Mountain came into view, and I counted how many times the radio towers blinked before I steered onto the dirt road that led to Peanut's compound.

When I parked in front of the gate, a pickup truck flashed its high beams at me, warning me to get off the property before we suffered the consequences. I imagined Peanut sent word not to engage me after my visit earlier in the day. If the driver recognized my face, I doubted he'd be getting out of his truck, but I'd sit here and wait if I needed to. Convincing Jessa to stay with the Bohannons hadn't been easy, but there was no more protected place in Tugalo County, and if things got hairy for me and Marshall, I wanted to know she was okay. A Tom Petty song started playing after Blue Oyster Cult faded out, and that's when I opened my door. I reached into the side pocket for my thumper, but the driver aimed an automatic rifle at me.

He hung half out of his window, his arms shaking from the gun's weight. The bill of an Atlanta Braves baseball cap hid his face, and I couldn't estimate his age by the sound of his voice, but I could hear some fear in it. He said I needed to back up and leave and not come back again, and I asked, "Peanut give you those orders, or are you trying to act like you got hair on your nuts?"

"It ain't got nothing to do with having hair on my nuts, Mack. I'm just doing what I'm told."

"It ain't fair you knowing who I am, and I can't see who you are."

"You ain't got to know who I am. Just do what I say."

"You and me are getting off on the wrong foot right now."

"I ain't asking you to dance. I'm telling you to leave."

"You wanna know what happens when someone gets off on the wrong foot with me?" I paused but didn't give him the chance to speak, "They end up getting their ass kicked."

"You got a gun aimed at you right now. I ain't afraid to shoot you."

"You ever shoot anybody before?"

He didn't answer.

"I have," I said. "I aimed a gun right between a preacher's eyes and blew his brains right outta his head. Took a week before I quit tasting that man's blood, and I still see his face every time I close my eyes. If you plan on shooting me, you better be prepared to lose a buncha goddamn sleep because I'll haunt you 'til the day you die."

Jessa took my hand in hers, squeezing it tight. Molly Hatchet played on the radio, and it was the only sound getting made besides our breathing until Marshall burst out laughing. He hung out the passenger's side window, banging on my truck door the way he would if he drummed on a set of congas, and said, "Yall done swinging your peckers around, or what?"

The gunman finally dropped his aim, slid back behind the wheel, opened his door, and got out of his truck. "That you, Marshall? Where the hell you been?"

"It don't make a damn where I been, Ricky. All that matters is that I'm here."

"Peanut know you back?"

"Not yet. He will as soon as you open that gate."

Ricky kicked a foot in the dirt, the automatic rifle dangling by his side. "I don't know that I oughta do that. He got real pissed when Brent Ford let Mack in."

"I didn't give Brent Ford no other choice."

"Shut up, Coy," Marshall said, then, "Peanut'll be happy to see me. I'll make sure Mack don't act no fool."

"Listen, Marshall," Ricky used the cap bill to scratch the back of his head, "if it weren't nobody but you, I'd be happy to let you in. Probably wouldn't have to ask Peanut neither. But your brother there caused all kinds of hell this morning. Brent Ford ain't gonna walk right for a long time. Might even have to have a surgery or two."

Marshall shot me a fighting look from the passenger's seat and said out the window, "Ricky, how 'bout you ask for me? See what Peanut has to say."

"All right," Ricky said, unclipping a walkie from his belt, "but if Peanut says no, yall are gonna have to leave."

Ricky turned his back on us, keying the radio, and talked so long I reckoned we'd end up spending the night out here, but he made his way over to the gate after speaking with Peanut, and said, "Yall can go on up."

4.

Peanut sat in one of his rocking chairs, waiting for us to park. Buford sat beside him, tall like an angry king after hearing news of his queen's unfaithfulness. A sable-coated German Shepherd I never saw before laid at Peanut's feet, its tail whipped back and forth, drumming a spasmodic rhythm on the floorboards. It lifted its head from its paws when we got out of the truck, a low growl trembling in its throat when we approached. Peanut spoke a command to the dog I couldn't hear, and it laid its head back down, not making another sound.

Buford stopped rocking his chair and leaned forward, squinting to get a better look at us in the dark. Peanut did the same but lumbered to his feet and came to stand at the edge of the front porch steps, the German Shepherd following him there and taking a seat next to him. Peanut looked past me and said, "What the hell you doing here?"

I could feel Marshall's smile when he said, "Well, I got to missing your face."

"Now ain't the time for you to be no smartass," Peanut said. "Something happen?"

"They got Mama, Peanut." Marshall stepped around me and walked to the bottom step. The porch light shined on my brother, and he became the center of attention, like some Broadway actor reciting a critical monologue. "Me and Mack's gotta get her back."

"Yall two need to let me handle everything. These ain't some fuckers you can take on by yourselves."

I spoke before my brother could. "We ain't got time to sit around and wait for you to handle your business, Peanut. Who knows what they're gone do now that they got Mama."

Peanut snarled at me, and Buford spat. "Don't go causing a buncha trouble I'll have to get you out of, Mack. I 'bout done you all the favors I'm willing to do. Ain't even cashed in on none of 'em yet either."

I pointed at Buford. "If they got your deddy right there, would you be waiting for me to handle business, or would you go get him yourself? How 'bout if it was Katie? Or Ray? Or Riley or Ramsey?"

Peanut lowered his voice, speaking in a murder-filled tone. "You best start keeping my boys' names outta yer mouth, Mack."

"He ain't meaning nothing by it, Peanut," Marshall said. "He's just trying to express the importance of what's happened. They got our mama. We can't just sit around doing nothing."

Peanut set his eyes back on Marshall. "It ain't that I'm asking yall to sit around and do nothing, all right? This gang is causing me all kindsa hell, and it's taking everything I got to keep it together. One more strand comes loose, and I might lose everything my deddy and granddeddy built."

"Peanut," I said, speaking over Marshall's shushes. "How 'bout you worry 'bout your business, and we'll worry 'bout our mama. Whatever it takes for us to get her back might end up helping you anyway."

"How can I make myself more clearly, Mack?"

"You can't," I said, "but there is something you can do for me. Keep an eye on Jessa while we're off in the weeds."

"This ain't no daycare service here," Buford spoke for the first time, his voice sounding like worn-out brakes grinding on rotors.

"Ain't nobody here speaking to you, old man."

Buford stiffened, said, "Speak to me in that manner one more time, and I'll teach you some respect Walter never did."

"Get inside, Deddy," Peanut punched a finger at the front door. "Now."

Buford rocked backward, the chair whining when he did, and Peanut waited, making sure he didn't speak again. After some silence spread over us, the dog filling it with an open-mouthed yawn, Peanut came down the steps, stopping midway down. He gave Jessa a flat smile but kept his eyes on me. "Nothing against yer woman there, Mack, but Deddy's right. I ain't running no daycare service. I got enough problems I'm worrying about, and I can't go adding yers to 'em."

"Peanut," I said, my voice even, "my Mama wouldn't be getting held hostage right now if it wasn't for you."

"I said I'd take care of it."

"That ain't good enough."

Jessa spoke, her voice slicing through the tension. "Hey, Mack, if Peanut don't wanna do this, then don't get in no argument with him over it. I'd rather stay with you anyway."

"We ain't getting in no argument," I said. "Peanut knows he owes me."

"I don't owe you shit, Dooley."

"Hey, Coy," Marshall said. "How 'bout you let me do the talking now."

Peanut spun when the front door opened, and Katie stepped outside. Her flip-flops smacked the bottoms of her feet as she crossed the porch, coming to stand above her husband. She'd grown her hair out since the last time I saw her and looked pretty, the darkness unable to keep it a secret. Her presence drew eyes to her the way a bug zapper attracts mosquitoes, and Peanut got demure.

Katie acted like us men didn't exist and spoke to Jessa. "Girl, how you been doing? I can't remember the last time I saw you. It was in town at Fat Mama's, wasn't it? I think we were both getting breakfast or something. Why don't you come on inside with me? I don't get to have friends over as much as I want. The boys playing sports and all that now takes up all my time. It'll be nice to have another lady over for a few days. I get tired of being outnumbered by all these tough guys."

Peanut deflated after Katie invited Jessa inside but didn't argue. He knew better. The whores at the Honey Suckle Ranch might do his bidding, and men from Scorpion Hollow might run drugs and guns across state lines for him, but Katie ran his house. His criminal empire ended inside her home's four walls.

Jessa didn't hesitate to break away from me either. She kissed me on the lips and whispered, "Please don't go and get yourself hurt," then spun on a heel and followed Katie inside.

Buford laughed when the front door shut and said, "Guess that settles that."

5.

We rode in silence after we left Peanut's; the only sound was the wind barreling outside the windows. Now that I didn't have to worry about Jessa's safety, my mind focused on Mama, hoping we could rescue her before the Ghostface Devils hurt her and that this didn't turn out the way it did with Andy.

My thoughts began spiraling after considering darker possibilities and my yearnings for a drink made me antsy. I drummed my fingers on the steering wheel and couldn't sit still in my seat, shifting my weight this way and that, resting an elbow on the center console or hanging an arm out of the door.

When I got to be a distraction to Marshall, he turned to me and asked, "You all right, Coy?"

"I'm good."

We didn't speak again. I followed winding blacktop further into North Georgia, where the Blue Ridge foothills turned into mountains and the air cooled by a few degrees. The roads got too sharp for me to speed up here, but slowing down let me appreciate the scenery, even at night. It'd been months since I'd come up this way. Our Uncle Arlo owned a cabin in these mountains we planned on spending the night at. No one would know to find us here, and we could hide out for at least one night.

I slowed my truck to a crawl, not wanting to miss the hidden drive, but I almost did anyway. Arlo hardly visited Tugalo County anymore; if he did, he never made us aware of his presence. The gravel road leading to his home hadn't gotten tended to in years, and parts of it had got washed out, and my truck bottomed out in ruts. Once we got to the cabin, Marshall hopped out before I could get the truck parked and disappeared around a corner. I waited at the front door until he opened it for me.

The living room smelled the way musty bed sheets do, and I left the door open to air it out. Marshall flipped a switch, providing us with some dingy light to see by.

"Guess Arlo's still paying the power bill," Marshall said.

I moved past my brother, bee-lining my way to Arlo's liquor cabinet, stocked with a collection of bourbons, despite my uncle's absence. I studied those bottles the same way Indiana Jones fretted over which chalice might be the Holy Grail. My thoughts got so consumed with what my nightcap would be that I didn't notice Marshall step behind me.

"I think you oughta leave the booze alone, Coy."

I wheeled around on my brother, the speed with which I moved caught him by surprise, and I punched him in the mouth. He stumbled backward, a hand reaching for his lips, smearing blood across his fingertips, and his eyes turned into a pair of livid thunderheads. Seeing anger flicker in his pupils like lightning streaks flashing across a violent sky made my body get electric. Before I could get control of myself, I lunged forward and met my brother in the center of the cabin.

We traded punches like prizefighters, our clenched fists

landing thumping blows in the ribs, shoulders, bellies, and jaws. When I got too dizzy to stand, I dove for Marshall's knees and drug him to the dusty floor. We rolled around, pinching, biting, and yanking each other's hair, cussing and cursing the other brother's existence. My brother got the better of me when he jacked a knee into my ballsack, my whole body bursting as though an atomic bomb got detonated inside me.

I rolled onto my back, knees crossed and clutching my member, coughing until I spasmed all over and couldn't see through my tears. Marshall scooted away from me until his back hit a wall and knuckled a streak of blood from his nose. Those thunderheads still stormed in his sockets, and if I wanted another round, he'd be ready for it, but I didn't have any fight left.

"You want a drink so bad you're starting fights over it, Coy? Go ahead," Marshall waved at the liquor cabinet, "be my guest. But you ain't gone be a damn bit useful to me or Mama if you're too liquored up to think."

I rolled onto my side, spat a pink snotball on the floor, and swiped a forearm across my eyes. Once my pain eased enough to move, I used an elbow to push myself upright and scooted over next to my brother. We didn't apologize to each other or extend any affection. We sat in silence until I finally broke it.

"Marshall, how'd all this bullshit come about?"

6.

Marshall elbowed himself off the wall, walked over to the liquor cabinet, and peered over the selection. He lifted a bottle or two, examined the labels and finally decided on some Maker's. It was Deddy's favorite whiskey, and if my brother didn't know what to drink, he went with what Deddy liked. He held the bottle up for me to see and said, "I guess we ort to have a drink."

He came over to me and reached a hand out for me to grab, and tentacles of pain twisted through my body when I got pulled upright. I followed Marshall into the kitchen, limping all the way, sat down at a table, and accepted a glass when he slid it to me. After he freed the cork from the bottle, Marshall gave us both a two-finger pour, and we drank without saying cheers.

The pain between my legs began to numb once the alcohol started circulating through my system, and I drained my glass on the second swallow. I reached across the table, seeing Marshall had barely taken a sip of his, and refilled my glass with a less generous pour than I would regularly take. This time I paced myself, sipping at the bourbon instead of taking guzzles, not wanting the haze to fog my mind too soon.

Marshall noticed the moderation I drank with now and asked, "You drinking yourself stupid every night, Coy?"

"My drinking habits ain't none of your business."

"You getting defensive like that tells me you are."

"This conversation is supposed to be about you and your dumbass decisions."

"Yeah," Marshall sipped on his whiskey, said, "at least I'm not in denial of mine."

Being confronted over my excess drinking made me want to slurp down my second pour and then chug the whole bottle. It's how I reacted to Jessa anytime she broached the subject, letting her know it wasn't up for discussion. Something about my brother bringing it up made me shove my glass into the middle of the table, doing so with such force that the brown liquor swirled over the rim and spilled on my hand. I wiped it clean on the front of my shirt and slumped in my chair the way a child does when they get told they can't have a cookie before supper.

"This is the only other thing I'm going to say about you drinking." Marshall slid his glass over next to mine. "These Ghostface Devils ain't some trailer park gangbangers. This ain't something they're doing for fun. They're dangerous motherfuckers, and if we go after them with you half-drunk, it'll get Mama killed."

Visions of Andy lying dead in the baptismal tub flashed before my eyes. Snakes coiled around her arms and legs, their tongues darting in and out of their mouths. Their hisses buzzed in my ears, getting so loud that I covered them with my palms. A cold sweat washed over me, and it got hard to breathe. No matter how much air I gulped into my lungs, it didn't seem like enough, and I pictured myself strapped to the weight bench, a towel yanked over my face, and a jug of water poured down my throat.

Marshall asked if I was okay, but I couldn't choke out the words. I sat there with my head between my knees until the world got back to normal and said, "I'll cut back on how much I'm drinking, but I can't stop. Not all the way."

Marshall nudged my glass over to me, and I reached for it, nursing a small sip from the glass and evening myself out.

Marshall said, "Take baby steps, Coy. Just don't let your drinking get in the way of helping Mama."

"I won't."

"Good enough," he said, reaching for his glass and sipping. "Last year, when Peanut sent me and Caudell up to Memphis, he wanted us to help Butcher Blake move some guns down to Atlanta. Blake's got a nephew down there who moves them throughout the city and gives Peanut a cut since it's technically his territory. What we didn't know is the Ghostface Devils have started moving out of the prisons."

"What do you mean?"

"They're a gang outta Sweetwater, Coy. I went and saw Deddy and asked him about 'em. Told me to get my ass back here and forget what Peanut wanted me to do. Never seen him get so scared over something. Damn near made me piss myself seeing him get that way. He got all bug-eyed and started shaking all over. Thought he might start crying. First thing I did after talking to Deddy was go to Caudell and tell him everything, but you know how he is. Ain't got an ounce of fear in him. He got hard as fuck and said he wouldn't let a buncha crackerjack white boys get him scared. Wasn't nothing I could say to that, so I didn't argue."

"What ended up happening?"

"The worst thing that possibly could."

I raised my eyes from the floor and looked at my brother sitting on the other side of the table. The muscles in his face got taut, and his eyes narrowed until it looked as though he'd dozed off. His lips flattened into a crease, and he spoke with a darkened tone. "They got Blake's nephew. Somehow or other, they found out where he stayed at and broke in during the night. They beat the shit outta that boy until he couldn't do nothing but raise a finger. Made his girlfriend watch, and once he couldn't fight back no more, they took her. When the law found her, she wasn't nothing but a mangled mess. Wouldn't even let her family peek at the corpse. Didn't kill Xay, though. Not right away."

Marshall paused, drained the rest of his glass, and got the bottle for a refill. He didn't speak again until he downed the entire second pour. "Coy, what I'm fixing to tell you is some fucked up shit, and I ain't never gone speak of it again. I can't stop having nightmares of what they did to that boy. I'd scrub my brain raw if it meant I could wipe my memory clean of the whole damn thing."

A shiver spread through Marshall, and his body got stiff, but he closed his eyes and breathed in long even breaths until he could go on. "Caudell got this call one night telling us to meet the Ghostface Devils at this warehouse we knew of. It was in some neutral territory where none of us would fight. They knew what they were doing getting us to show up there. Told us not to come by until late in the evening after all the businesses closed. Soon as we rolled onto the property, shit didn't feel right. It was just something in the air, ya know? Like all the electrodes or whatever the fuck was wrong."

Marshall reached for his empty glass but shoved it away, sat a grim pair of eyes on me, and went on with his story. "They crucified him, Coy, and I ain't fucking around when I say that. Stripped his ass naked and nailed him upside down, but that wasn't even the worst fucking part. Somehow, they fastened a bucket around his head, filled it up with lighter fluid, and set him on fire. I can't get the smell outta my nose. Don't make a damn what I do. Every time I take a breath of air, it smells like overcooked bacon."

"Goddamn."

"Goddamn is right. Caudell went into a frenzy that scared the shit outta me. Damn near as bad as that crucifixion. He went on the warpath, and I followed suit. I was too scared not to. We tracked down every piece of shit we could find and didn't just kill 'em, we murdered 'em, and did it in such gruesome ways it couldn't be considered human, but Caudell wanted to make sure once they got to Hell, the Devil wouldn't recognize who he was fucking. We'd still be killing them boys, too, if Peanut hadn't intervened. His contacts in the government down there got ahold of him and told him about the war going on. Made us pull outta Atlanta and disappear, so here I am."

7.

I drank until my brain lost its ability to conjure dreams and went to bed. Sleep came over me in a rush, and I didn't move until my brother woke me. He stood over me in a pair of Arlo's clothes and told me to get ready. Muddy water sprayed out of the tub faucet and didn't get any cleaner after I turned on the shower. I gave myself a rinse and dressed in the clothes I wore the day before.

Marshall got some coffee brewing and sat at the kitchen table waiting for me. I sat down across from him and shoved the empty bottle of Maker's out of my line of sight. The smell of coffee brewing made my belly grumble, and I couldn't recall when I last ate. I needed to fill it with something, so I got up and started searching the cabinets.

Marshall said, "Arlo ain't got nothing in there that ain't a canned good or done expired. We'll have to go into town and get something to eat."

"Let's do it as soon as the coffee's done making. I'd eat a donkey's asshole if you threw it on a plate in front of me right now."

"I hear asshole is pretty good if you smother it with some Duke's."

"You know Duke's improves the flavor of almost anything. Even pickles."

We both took our coffee black and rode with the windows down. The crisp air dried our hair and cleared out thoughts from the night before. Imagining some kid getting crucified rattled me near as bad as the evil done to Andy. Remembering Marshall's descriptions made my coffee taste bland, and I wished I'd spiked it with some bourbon.

Once we got into town, I hit the drive-through line at Fat Mama's Southern Kitchen and ordered us both a couple of biscuits. After getting our food, we found an empty space and ate without speaking. My belly calmed down some after finishing my first biscuit and quit complaining after eating the second. Marshall tossed our trash into a can outside his window, and we sat there, drinking our coffee.

"I ain't got no idea where they're keeping Mama," Marshall said, "but I do know where some of them pecker warts stay at."

I drank the last of my coffee and poured the dregs out the window. "Think we oughta go pay 'em a visit and see what they know?"

"I imagine they'd appreciate the company."

I shifted the truck into reverse and backed out of the parking spot. My cellphone buzzed, leaving Fat Mam's, and I checked the screen to see it was Monty. I let him go to voice mail, and after he left his message, I flipped the phone open to see four missed calls. One was from Peanut, who didn't leave a message, and the rest were from Monty. I dialed the code that got me into my messages and listened to Monty ask what bug got up my ass and why I avoided him. I flipped the phone shut after his voice went off the line and tossed the phone onto the seat.

"Everything all right?"

"It's just work."

"Oh yeah? Mama said you started coaching for the Titans."

"Yeah, if that's what you wanna call babysitting a buncha mamas and deddys who think their kids are All-SEC."

"Shit."

Marshall told me to head for Lake Ayers, and then he'd give me directions from there. It was a good day to be out on the water, and plenty of families enjoyed it. Speed boats pulled tubers behind them, and pontoons floated about while kids dove off the sides. Jessa had been telling me for a week or two now that she wanted to spend a day on the lake, but I couldn't set my bottle down long enough to take her. Guilt upset my belly at the thought, and I wanted to gag up my breakfast.

Marshall distracted me from thinking of how I mistreated my girlfriend by telling me to take the road leading to the Ida River Trail. The trail was closed because of some flooding during the spring, but most of the roads people lived on were still driveable. We drove down dirt roads in such poor condition I couldn't give the accelerator more than a tap and got so deep in the woods I expected to hear banjos twang at any moment.

Most roads out here were unmarked, and the only way of knowing where we were was by remembering where the trail was. I'd already got so turned around a compass couldn't have got me back on track, but Marshall didn't seem one bit lost. He leaned against the door with a sharp eye on the road and told me to find somewhere to park. I found a spot leading into some beech trees and pulled far enough offroad so my truck wouldn't get spotted.

"They live in a trailer down a road right over there,"

Marshall pointed toward a bunch of overgrowth. "We can't drive it cause they'll know we're coming. We'll have to hike the rest of the way."

"How many people are living down in there?"

"No more than two or three, but we'll want to stake it out just to be sure."

"I'd rather not get shot all to hell, Marshall."

"Then we'll need to use the element of surprise, Coy."

Marshall shoved his door open before I could argue any further and waited for me at the front of the truck. I got out and grabbed the thumper before shutting the door and saw my brother's face twist with surprise.

"Where the hell'd you find Deddy's thumper at?"

"Found it going through some of his stuff Mama wanted to get rid of." I knocked the hitch ball against my boot heel. "Told her I was keeping it."

"You remember how he used to yell at us for playing with it?" Marshall laughed. "He'd get so damn mad over that."

"He thought we was gone bust our heads open. We never did, though."

"And that was more outta luck than anything else."

Marshall led me around a briar patch and got his boots tangled in some kudzu that didn't want to let him go. Sunrays kept our backsides warm, and my clothes started clinging to my arms and legs. Our hike turned into more of a trek, and my coffee roiled around the inside of my belly. We came over a rise and saw the trailer sitting at the bottom of a holler. A truck was parked around the back, and a dirt bike lay on its side. Heavy metal music blared from an open window, letting us know somebody was at home.

I squatted to my heels next to Marshall, and we spent some time watching the place. Nobody came or went while we sat there or changed the music to something better. My quads started burning after squatting for so long, and I stood up, prompting Marshall to follow my lead. He used his shirt to towel the sweat from his eyes and asked, "What are you thinking?"

"That their damn music is getting on my nerves."

"They could be listening to something worse."

"Like what?"

"I don't know." Marshall shrugged. "A cat getting run over or some shit like that."

I nodded but didn't tell my brother I'd prefer to listen to a squawling cat.

8.

Getting down close to the trailer made me hesitant about going inside. It sat in such a state of disrepair that it looked as if it'd collapse from a strong gust of wind. Kudzu vines strangled a corner, causing it to sag on that side. The music blared from a busted-out window, and a Confederate Flag curtained it. I placed a foot on a rotten front porch step but didn't let all my weight down, ensuring it wouldn't give out under me. Once I knew it would hold, I made my way to a cock-eyed front door and tapped on it with the business end of the thumper.

No one came to answer because the goddamn noise played so loud it rattled the door in its frame. I knocked a second time, producing a loud thudding against the aluminum but still got left waiting outside and started worrying Marshall would get impatient and rush in without me. He'd gone around back and agreed not to bust in until I smashed the stereo. I planned on knocking one more time, and if no one answered, I'd invite myself in.

On the third knock, which consisted of me whopping the front door with the ball hitch, a kid who probably didn't have his diploma yet yanked it open. He stared at me with bloodshot eyes, and I took a step back after getting a whiff of his rotten odor. A tattoo of a bearded skull with glowing eyes wearing a Stars and Bars bandana with dragoon pistols crossed behind it covered most of his chest and torso. Bruises ran the lengths of his arms, and the words HELL YEAH were tattooed on his knuckles. He squinted at me after looking at the thumper and asked, "Who the hell are you?"

"I'm your neighbor."

"My neighbor?" His voice twisted up. "We ain't got no neighbors."

"Yeah, hoss, I live right over yonder." I pointed over my shoulder in no particular direction.

The kid looked around me, gazing off in the distance. When he set his eyes back on me, they glanced down at the thumper held by my side. "What you doing with that nigger knocker?"

"Strike one."

"Do what?"

"You only get one strike."

"You're getting me pissed off." The kid snarled, and it let me see a mouth full of decaying teeth. "What do you want?"

"I walked over here to let you know your taste in music sucks."

"The fuck?" The kid spat the words out. "Get the fuck outta here 'fore I yank that nigger knocker outta your hand and beat you with it."

"What'd I tell you?"

"You ain't told me shit."

"I said you only get one strike."

"Or what, motherfuck—"

Before the kid could finish cussing, I smashed the hitch end of the thumper into his nose, flattening it like a squashed bug. Blood spewed over his cheeks and mouth, and the kid couldn't keep upright. He stumbled backward, sitting down hard on moldy carpet, covering his broken sniffer with both hands, trying his best to stanch the blood flow. With him no longer blocking the entryway, I invited myself inside, found the stereo sitting on a plastic children's table, rared back, and smashed the hell out of it. The assault on my ears ended, and they finally got sweet relief.

"What the fuck?" A voice hollered, and I turned to see my long-haired friend standing in the kitchen. He wore nothing but a soiled pair of tighty-whities, and prison ink covered his lank frame from neck to ankles. I only got an eye blink to study the racist emblems before he aimed a pistol aimed at my chest, and he said, "I told Meyer I'd be the one who got to shoot you."

"Who's Meyer?"

"You ain't got to worry 'bout it now," he said, letting out a whoop. "Too bad that bitch of yours ain't here to watch. I'll go see her again, though. Guaran-damn-tee it."

I tightened my grip on the thumper, my knuckles straining from it. "You better watch your mouth when you talk about her."

"What the fuck are you gonna do when I got a gun aimed in your face?"

"Stand here and watch."

"You damn sure are," he said, waving the pistol around.

I stepped to the side, outside his aim, and raised my voice until I damn near yelled, "You ain't understanding me. I'm fixing to watch my brother whoop your ass."

"Do what?"

Marshall flung the backdoor open, barreling into the trailer and charging the Ghostface Devil the way a bull charges a matador. I spun on my heel when I caught a glimpse of movement from the corner of my eye and bashed the kid's ribcage with the thumper. He fell in a heap next to me, and I struck him again to ensure he wouldn't get up.

"Goddamn, Coy," Marshall said, standing over the Ichabod with the pistol shoved into the waist of his jeans, "I bet his mama felt that."

"She ought to for raising such a piece of shit."

"What do you wanna do with 'em now?"

9.

When we got back to Arlo's cabin, Marshall worked on getting Ichabod tied to a chair while I fixed myself a drink. I liked drinking my bourbon on the rocks, but there weren't any ice trays in the freezer, so I drank it neat. It made the alcohol burn brighter when I swallowed and the haziness set in quicker, so I limited myself to a snort. I heard the Ghostface Devil start groaning when he began regaining consciousness, and a string of cuss words followed. I added a small shot to my empty glass and knocked it back before returning to the living room.

Ichabod's eyes danced around the room until they found me, and the muscles throughout his chest and arms flexed, rippling the way still waters do when rocks get skipped across the surface. He opened his mouth to speak, but Marshall stretched a nylon bungee cord across it, securing the ends together and twisting until Ichabod's lips pulled back in a rictus smile. Now he yowled the way a pair of tomcats do when they're fighting over territory.

Marshall stepped away from him, shaking his head, and said, "I ain't gone be able to listen to this shit for long."

"I ain't in no mood for it either."

"What do you wanna do with him then?" Marshall asked and jabbed a stiff finger into one of Ichabod's ears, shoving it in knuckle deep, as though he meant to finger-bang ol' buddy's brain.

"You hungry?"

"I could have a bite." Marshall smiled now and just poked at Ichabod for the sake of being annoying.

"Let's go grab something to eat while he gets all that nonsense outta his system."

"Think he'll be all right here by himself?"

"How good did you tie them knots?"

Marshall winked and said, "Brystal taught me how to tie these knots right here, Coy. I ain't gone tell you why she taught 'em to me, but I'll say this, he'll lose a damn wrist 'fore he gets out of 'em."

"Whatever, Marshall." I scooped my keys off a table and headed for the door.

"Hey, now," Marshall said, "there ain't nothing wrong with some kinkiness in the bedroom. You and Jessa oughta try it sometime."

I used the steering wheel to pull myself into the seat and waited for Marshall to get inside. He pulled the door to and stood on the front porch until I honked the horn. When he got in the truck, I asked, "What was you doing?"

"Listening to him holler."

"How come?"

"Making sure it wasn't too loud."

I cranked the truck, said, "We can't be wasting too much time grabbing food."

"Let's just grab a bucket of chicken from the Dixie Mart and come on back."

When I got a mile or two down the road, I shifted around in my seat, getting uncomfortable from a question bouncing around my thoughts. Marshall noticed how I couldn't sit still and asked, "What's done got into you, Coy? Acting like you got a turtle head poking out or something."

I inhaled until my lungs got so full of oxygen that it made me hope the question would get forced out with the outburst of air. When I exhaled, nothing but silence followed, and I sat behind the wheel until the Dixie Mart came into view. Marshall sat next to me when I shifted into park and waited for me to finally speak. I asked, "What going on with you and Brystal?"

"That's a helluva question to get so nervous over."

"There's something worse we gotta talk about."

"Oh hell."

I shook my head. "Get the small stuff outta the way first. I ain't told you how I went and saw her the other day. She damn near bit my head off when I asked about you."

"We ain't on such good terms right now, Coy." Marshall sniffed and brushed the back of an arm across his nose. "That might've been the last you ever saw of her."

"How come?"

"That relationship's done run its course, I guess."

"There's more to it than that."

Marshall shrugged. "There really ain't. She just wants more than I can give her."

"What's that?"

"Marriage and kids and a happy home. The way I see it, that's always been your thing. I'm just here to have a good time, and if a woman wants to stick around for it, then good for her."

"Brystal's always been good to you."

"Yeah," Marshall said, opening his door, "but that don't mean I oughta change my ways for her."

"Get me a Co-Cola, would ya?"

He nodded.

On the way back to Arlo's cabin, Marshall asked, "What's the something worse you said we needed to talk about?"

I steered onto the cabin's dirt drive and let the truck coast. I'd forgotten all about me saying that when I got a sniff of the fried chicken. It smelled the way Sundays do, and it got my mouth watering. All I thought about on the drive back to Arlo's was the first bite I'd take from a chicken thigh, but now my mind turned to darker things.

I said, "You know we can't let this boy live, right?"

"Hell, I thought we should've killed the one we left back at the trailer."

"He was just a kid, Marshall."

"And you think that makes a damn why?"

I ran a hand over my face, scrubbing at my beard when I did. "Killing someone that young just doesn't sit right with me."

"Shit, he wouldn't have blinked twice about killing you."

The thought got me sick. "I don't wanna have to think about him. It's Ichabod we're talking 'bout here."

Marshall burst out laughing. "Who the fuck is Ichabod?"

"That's the nickname I gave to ol' dude. He looks like the character from that Disney cartoon."

"All right," Marshall shrugged. "What we gone do with Ichabod afterward?"

"Arlo's got plenty of property he can disappear on."

"Hauling a body around all this land is gone be a bitch."

I parked my truck next to the cabin. "What do you think we oughta do?"

"Bonfire."

"That'll let someone know we're here."

"Dammit, Coy." Marshall smacked the dashboard. "Let's not make no damn mess."

10.

We sat in the truck, eating our chicken, and watched the sky change colors. When we got out, it had turned a shade of sandstone, and the sun retreated behind the Blue Ridge Mountains. Soon enough, it'd get dark, and I imagined neither of us would be getting a good night's sleep. Not with Mama's fate in Ichabod's hands. Thoughts of me failing Andy filled my mind; I got jittery and started yearning for a drink to loosen me up.

Marshall stopped at the front porch steps and said, "We need to decide who's gone do what?"

"What do you mean?"

"I mean, whose gone be the one asking the questions and who's gone be the triggerman."

"I'm gone be the one asking the questions."

"Who the hell put you in charge?"

"I just figured that's how it'd go since I'm older."

"Well, it ain't," Marshall said, clenching his fists.

"Don't get your pecker in a knot, Marshall." I slapped him on the shoulder. "I'm just kidding."

Marshall stuck his fist out. "Rock paper scissors."

"Do what?"

"That's how we'll decide."

"Damn, we ain't thirteen no more."

"Stick it out there, Coy."

I stuck my fist out, and we shook them the way someone does when throwing dice, showing our picks when Marshall called shoot. We both chose rock.

"Do it again," Marshall said.

Throughout our childhood, we played this game to decide who would get stuck with the shitty chores. Neither of us wanted to spend the weekend at Mammaw's and get scratched all to hell because she wanted her cats to get a bath. Marshall never knew he had a tell that let me know his pick. Whenever he'd squint, he'd choose paper, and if he stuck his tongue out, he picked scissors. He got stoic if he chose rock.

I watched his face while we shook our fists, and he started squinting. When he called shoot, I chose scissors.

"Sumbitch," he said. "Best two-out-of-three."

"Nope. You lost fair and square."

"Goddammit, Coy, c'mon."

"We're wasting time, Marshall," I said, walking up the steps.

"Dammit all to hell. I ain't fixing to be the one who gets stuck cleaning up the mess, you hear me?" Marshall said, coming up behind me. "I got stuck doing all that shit with Caudell, and you ain't fixing to do the same with me."

I stopped at the front door and turned to face my brother. "Whatever mess gets made, we clean it up together."

Marshall exhaled, and I watched tension get released from his shoulders and chest. He punched my arm, said, "You're scooping up all his brains."

"If he's even got any," I said, opening the front door.

Ichabod's eyes cut over to me, the corners of his mouth bleeding from the bungee cord cutting into them, and squealed the way a pig does when they get picked up off the ground. He jerked against his restraints, rocked his chair all around, and came within a frog's hair of tipping it over. I pointed my finger at him and said, "You knock yourself over, and I'm gone bust your brains in."

Ichabod tried cussing at me, but the bungee cord stifled the words.

I made my way for the kitchen, but Marshall hung back. "Where you going, Coy?"

"Gotta grab something real quick. You want anything to drink?"

"Naw, I'm good."

In the kitchen, I filled my glass with a half-pour of bourbon, drinking most of it right there on the spot. My jitters eased up on me some but didn't go away. Getting information of Mama's whereabouts still left me with some shakes, and trying to drink those away would only get me drunk. I topped off my drink before grabbing my thumper off the table, and when I came back into the living room, Ichabod's face puckered with fear when he heard me dragging the ball hitch on the floor.

Marshall walked over behind him, and I came right up to him, sipping my drink. I knocked the hitch against my boots the way a ballplayer does when they're next at-bat, and clumps of dirt got knocked loose from the tread. Ichabod took up a pleading tone, but the bungee cord made him sound pathetic. I sat my glass on the closest table, cupped my hand around my ear, and said, "Sorry, what'd you say? I can't understand you when you're talking with your mouth full."

He went back to squealing, and I motioned at Marshall

to let him loose. Once he felt slack in the bungee cord, Ichabod spat it out, and drool spilled from his mouth. Long strings of saliva ran down the tattoos covering his chest and gleamed in the dusty lighting. When he spoke, it was in between great gulps of air. "You . . . two . . . are so fucked. Hurt me all yall want, but it won't have shit on how the Ghostface Devils retaliate. We'll start with yall's Mama and make yall watch. The both of yall will have nightmares of what we do to her before we finally put yall out of your misery."

Marshall whopped him upside his head, snapping it forward, and made his eyes dance in their sockets. Ichabod blinked them hard to regain his focus. When he did, I got down in his face, tapping the thumper on the floor next to his feet, and let him get a good look at me. Once I saw thoughts forming in his eyes, I said, "The next time you mention my mama, I want you telling me where she's at. You threaten her safety again, and I'll make you eat this fucking hitch."

Ichabod spat in my face, and I recoiled, tasting his dirty mouth in mine. I snatched my bourbon glass off the table, spilled some of it on the floor, and drank until his flavor got burned from my taste buds. After I emptied my glass, I returned it to the table, wiped my mouth with the back of my arm, and said, "You can forget about me being nice to you now."

"Fuck off," Ichabod said.

"You ain't in no position to demand that."

"I'm gonna slit your throat and make your girlfriend piss in the hole."

"You'll be dead before you get the chance."

Ichabod screamed in my face, and I did it back to him. The sound of tree frogs singing filled the cabin after our voices gave out. I stepped back before he thought to spit another loogie in my face and lifted the thumper to eye level. "I'm fixing to ask you three questions. You lie to me or don't answer me at all, and I'll knock the ever-loving shit outta you."

"Fuck off," Ichabod said again.

"Let's start with an easy question." I smiled. "What's your name?"

Ichabod cocked his head to the side, looking at me with a hostile expression, and said, "My name is whatever I want it to be."

I struck the space between his feet with the thumper, banging it off the hardwood floor, and Ichabod jumped in his seat and would've tipped over if Marshall hadn't been standing there to keep him upright. He let out a bark that I spoke over, "Pick a fucking a name, or it'll be one of your toes next time."

"I'm gonna make sure you're screaming out my name while you're dying." He leaned forward in the chair until his restraints pulled tight.

I bent at the waist, said, "I can't scream it out if I don't know it, dumbass."

His hostile face turned militant, and he dropped his voice low. "Shane."

"Say it again."

"You heard me."

I bashed a spot next to Shane's foot, giving his smallest toe a glancing blow. His body jolted as if an electrical current surged through it and hollered the way a little child does when they get their tail whooped. I watched his face, waiting for the pain in his expression to diminish before I spoke again. "Say your name louder this time, or I'll break that toe."

Shane inhaled until his chest swelled the way a balloon does when it's on the verge of popping and when he exhaled, his name rode the outburst of air.

"Hey, Marshall," I said, looking over Shane and at my brother, "if your name can be whatever you choose, why would you pick something stupid like Shane?"

Marshall grinned, said, "These Ghostface Devils are all pecker and no brains, Coy." Marshall leaned forward, looking over Shane's shoulder. "And that's saying something because from what I heard, they ain't got a whole lotta pecker."

"Fuck you both," Shane said, snarling at us. "I'll carve my fucking name on both your chests."

I swung the thumper, pretending to practice my downswing. "You talk a whole lotta shit for someone tied to a chair."

Shane didn't respond, but his facial expression betrayed him. The militant look he wore slipped and let me see his fear.

"Now that we got our introductions outta the way," I said, "how 'bout we move onto question number two." I put up two fingers, forming a peace sign. "You mentioned some ol' boy by the name of Meyer back at your trailer. Tell me all I need to know about him."

Shane tried mustering a laugh, but it came out sounding like a honk. "Meyer's the man who's gonna kill you," he said, his voice getting high-pitched and spooky.

"I thought you said you were gone kill us." I pointed the hitch at him, acting confused.

"You'll wish it was me," Shane said, spitting all over himself. "Meyer's the one who enjoys killing. He'll take his time and get off on your suffering. He's got a wire or two crossed and will come up with the most disturbing shit to do to you."

I shrugged. "Can't be no worse than some of the things I let Beth Ann Bowman do to me a few summers back. That's the kinda girl you see in some movies you don't want your mama to know you're watching."

"Joke about it all you want. Meyer will have you wishing you were dead."

"We'll see about all that." I went back to practicing my downswing. "You ain't answered my question, though. Who is Meyer?"

"He's the Grim Reaper."

"All right," I said, turning to Shane, "I'm tired of all these bullshit answers. You tell me who Meyer is, or I'm breaking your ankle."

"Break it, motherfucker."

"Goddamn, we got a brave one here, Marshall."

"Told ya, Coy," Marshall said, grabbing the back of the chair, "more pecker than brains."

I lined up next to Shane's ankle like I was getting ready to tee off at Augusta National Golf Club, going through a few practice swings the way John Daly would before striking the ball. Shane pinched his eyes shut, not wanting to see the coming blow, and bit back a scream that escaped through his rotting teeth. When I rared back to tee off on his ankle, his eyes burst open, and he hollered for me to wait.

"Stop," he yelled. "Stop! Stop! STOP!"

I pulled back on the thumper, the ball hitch an eyelash away from obliterating Shane's bones. "I hope you're fixing to tell me everything I wanna know."

Shane answered in an onslaught of words. "Meyer is the Leviathan. Runs everything from here to Sweetwater.

Whores, drugs, you name it. Ain't nobody's bad side you wanna get on worse than his."

"This is all Peanut's territory," Marshall said, pulling back on the chair and getting down in Shane's face.

Shane shook his head. "Not no more, it's not. The Ghostface Devils are moving in, and Peanut's fighting a losing battle."

"People been saying that about the Bohannons for a long time," I said. "That family is harder to exterminate than an intrusion of roaches."

Shane looked at me, his eyes ocean-deep and tumultuous. "The Ghostface Devils run Georgia now, and when we leave Tugalo County, there won't be a single Bohannon left."

I nodded. "What's a Leviathan?"

"Meyer is."

I swung the thumper overhead, the ball hitch aimed at the ceiling, ready to smash it between Shane's thighs and crack his nuts like a set of pecans. He jerked against his restraints, attempting to lift his hands and plead for me to stop, his muscles flexing until the veins bulged beneath the skin and corded up his arms and neck, forming a disjointed pattern.

"Leviathan just means he's third in command. They got these ranking among the Ghostface Devils, and Meyer's got Lucifer and Beelzebub above him. Them two are both in Sweetwater and run everything from there. They got life sentences and hand-picked Meyer to do their bidding on the outside. Trained him to run everything while he did a nickel with 'em. He's their boy."

Marshall set the chair back down on all fours, and I lowered the thumper to the floor and leaned on it like a hiking stick. We looked at each other, trying to sort the puzzle pieces into place without using words, but I couldn't get over the silly use of code names. "Yall are a buncha Dungeons and Dragons playing motherfuckers, ain't ya?"

Shane's words got sour, and he said, "I don't play none of that nerd-ass shit, you hear me? Changing this country ain't no game. Us Ghostface Devils will return the White man to his proper place. We believe in His purity and authority and that there ain't no person of color who oughta have any charge over him. There ain't a White man alive who oughta be siding with a lesser race. Do you understand how you're defiling yourself? It's a goddamn shame. But if that's gonna be your choice, get outta the fucking way or get steamrolled by men who believe in this cause."

I tapped the thumper on the floor, adding a backbeat rhythm to the song the tree frogs sang outside. "I remember this kid I went to school with by the name of Barry Wade. Barry was one of them good ol' boy types who came to school wearing the rebel flag on his back and talked all that White power shit. His deddy would run Klan rallies in their front yard and burn crosses for all the neighbors to see. It got in Barry's head, and he believed all the same shit you're saying down to his toes. At least he pretended to, anyway. You remember all this, Marshall?"

"It's starting to come back to me." Marshall nodded. "I remember Barry being a pussy, too."

"He was." I laughed. "Talked up a whole pile of shit to get people mad and stirred up but wouldn't never fight over his beliefs. I think he liked the attention more than anything else. He ended up getting it too. Not the kind he wanted, though. See, Barry always did his talking in front of big crowds with plenty of adult supervision around.

Teachers would always break everything up and tell Barry to keep his damn mouth shut. Well, one day, us boys on the football team decided we'd take care of Barry. I can't remember all the details, but we got Barry down in the visitors' locker room because we didn't want his stank ass stepping into ours and beat that boy's ass into a piece of meatloaf. Stuffed him inside a locker and left him there for the janitors to find. Didn't see him in school for weeks, but when he came back, he didn't talk no more of that shit."

"Nope," Marshall said, his hands resting on the back of Shane's chair. "Came back to school acting like Mahatma Gandhi."

Shane lowered his voice until he spoke right above a whisper. "I'm glad yall got to take this stroll down memory lane, but yall can't stop the storm that's coming."

"Shane, you know what a weatherman gets paid to do?" I said but didn't wait for him to ask. "Be wrong because all they ever are is wrong."

Shane's face screwed up. He raised his voice until he almost hollered. "The storm is coming, and when it gets here—"

"Shut the fuck up and tell me where my mama is."

He laughed now. Laughing until his chest heaved, the tattoos on his belly rolled, and his biceps flexed, his arms looking sculpted from bodybuilding. "Your mama is the least of your worries."

I paced the floor, unable to get his laughter out of my head. "You ever busted your shin on a trailer hitch, Shane?" I asked, holding the hitch end of the thumper a finger length from his eyes. He tried pulling away from the weathered piece of steel, but Marshall held his head in place. "It hurts like a sumbitch, don't it, Marshall?"

"Sure as hell does," Marshall said. "Still got a scar on my leg from the time I knocked it on one when I was five."

Without saying another word, I swung the thumper over my shoulder, the ball hitch cutting through the air with a whoosh, and brought it around with such force I almost lost my balance. Shane's screams filled my ears now with no evidence of the laughter or mockery that had been there moments before. Marshall leaned over him, struggling to keep the chair on all fours, and whooped in his face.

"Goddamn, Coy!" He said. "Another swing like that, and he'll be walking on a peg leg like Long John Silver."

I ignored Marshall, grabbing Shane's face and looking him in the eye. "Tell me where my mama is, or I'll break that fucking leg."

Lightning streaks brightened his pupils, and his words came out sounding like mush. "She'll be dead before you can get to her."

I stepped back, swiping the thumper over my shoulder, and brought it forward in a swift motion, striking Shane's leg right below my first shot. The sound reverberating through the cabin reminded me of crab leg dinners and how Deddy would use a mallet to pound meat from the claws. Shane's screams rang in my ears now, and he couldn't form words for the pain.

I waited for it to subside and asked, "What'd you say?"

"The church," he said, his teeth grinding together. "We're keeping her at the church."

"Where's the church at?"

"I can't tell you that."

I swung the thumper, and Shane flinch, but I brought it to rest on my shoulder. "I'm done fucking with you, Shane," I said. "If you ain't fixing to tell me what I wanna know, I'm gone let Marshall take over this questioning. Except if you don't answer him right, he's gone put a bullet through your brain."

"I can't tell you where the church is," Shane hollered. "I swear to God I can't. Meyer'll kill me if I do."

"You need to worry about us killing you."

"Death at your hands does not scare me."

"You believe that, Marshall?"

"Not a damn bit," Marshall said, stepping around the chair and pressing the pistol against Shane's temple. "You got 'til the count of three to tell me what I want to know."

"I won't. I fucking won't. But Meyer will kill you. Right after he kills—"

"Three," Marshall said, skipping the numbers that proceeded it and stained the cabin wall with Shane's gore.

11.

Shane's head lolled on his shoulder, the bullet hole leaking blood like water from a drippy faucet. A spatter pattern on the wall next to him captured my attention, and I stared at it, attempting to decipher the image. Marshall came around the chair, stood next to me, crossed his arms over his chest, and stared at the wall with me. A few heartbeats passed before our silence finally got broken.

"What you think it is?" Marshall asked.

I shifted my weight from one foot to the other, leaned on the thumper, and squinted. "I see a couple of different things, to be honest with you."

"Yeah," Marshall pointed, circling his finger around an area closest to the corner of the wall, "that spot right there reminds me of a Jackson Pollock painting."

I turned to my brother, looking at him with a critical eye.

He turned to me, confusion spreading across his features. "What?"

"Jackson fucking Pollock? What the fuck do you know about Jackson fucking Pollock?"

"Enough to know that spot right there," Marshall jabbed his finger at the wall, "reminds me of one of his paintings."

"You're just talking shit," I said. "I thought you were going to say it reminded you of a mountain range or a stroll through the woods. But Jackson fucking Pollock? Damn, Marshall."

"You're acting like a real asshole, Coy. I know a little 'bout this and that."

"Whatever." I tossed my thumper onto the couch and headed into the kitchen with Marshall following me. He rattled off some history about Pollock's career while I grabbed a pair of clean glasses from a cabinet and filled them both with double pours of bourbon. Marshall reached for his glass when I offered it to him and drank without saying cheers.

After we drained our whiskey and both got refills, Marshall said, "You know what I just thought of? We ort to have put a tarp down to make cleanup a whole lot easier."

I shrugged. "Ain't gone do us no good to stand here and think about what we should've done. We done did what we did."

"I know that," he said. "All I'm saying is if we ever get in this sorta situation again, these are the kinda things we ort to have on hand."

"What the hell do you plan on doing that will ever get us in another situation like this?"

"I ain't planning on doing shit, but sometimes life just happens."

I left my glass on the kitchen table and opened the cabinet under the sink, looking for any cleaning supplies Arlo might have. "You been standing in the wrong damn bumper sticker aisle, Marshall. This ain't what they mean when they say, 'sometimes life just happens.'"

I heard Marshall sit his glass on the kitchen table and walk over to stand next to me. He started lifting the bottles

I'd taken from the cabinet and placed them on the counter after reading their labels. "Ain't none of this stuff gone work here, Coy. It'll mess up them floors."

"That blood's gone mess 'em up worse if we don't find something soon."

"Arlo got any baking soda down there? I saw Caudell use that to clean some up one time."

I stuck my head inside the cabinet, searching for anything resembling a box of baking soda but didn't see nothing. "Check the fridge. See if Arlo's got some in there."

I used the countertop to pull myself from my knees, turned to catch a box Marshall tossed to me, flipped it over to check the best-by date, and found it to have passed three years ago. It would have to do because I didn't see either of us getting on our hands and knees and scrubbing blood from the floor with soap and water the way some Disney Princess would.

Marshall followed me toward the living room, and when I crossed the kitchen's threshold, a harsh light seared my vision, causing my eyes to burn in their sockets so that I saw nothing but shadows floating across the back of my lids. I used a forearm to block them from the light, but it did nothing to protect them.

I heard Marshall speak to me in an urgent tone, but his voice got drowned out by the spirit-filled preaching of Randy Jessup. The preacher's voice gave me sight, and I saw him sitting in Shane's place, the bullet hole in the middle of his head filling Arlo's tiny living room with a heavenly light my eyes couldn't tolerate without a divine touch. Scar tissue no longer covered his missing eye. It had healed, and now he looked at me with two brilliant pupils, a blue flame burning in the center of them, filling me with a sense of dread, which started churning in my stomach and pumped its way to the back of my throat.

The sight bent me over at the waist and I kept my balance by resting my hands on my knees, and dry heaved until tears shattered my vision into tiny shards and made me see Randy Jessup's face in each of them. His laughter filled my ears, and my mind vibrated until my thoughts got disarranged and incoherent. My gagging continued until strings of spit dangled from the corners of my mouth, and gastric acid burned my throat raw.

Marshall clapped me on the back the way our mammaw would when we got overcome by a coughing fit. It knocked me from the grip of the hallucination, my eyes readjusted to the dim lighting of Arlo's cabin, and I saw Shane's barren eyes staring at me. I began sweating icicles and shivered as though a cold front moved down from the Blue Ridge Mountains and settled in the hollers of Tugalo County.

"Damn, Coy, you all right?"

I couldn't respond to my brother for the way my throat seized up, and I shoved him away to give myself plenty of space to catch my breath. After refilling my lungs and standing up straight again, I retrieved the baking soda from where I dropped it on the floor and began sprinkling it on the blood puddle.

"You just gone act like that shit didn't happen?" Marshall asked.

Marshall's question got replaced by the droning of cicadas while I gathered the strength to answer. When I could speak, I said, "Let's not waste no more time and get rid of this body."

12.

After we got the blood cleaned up, Marshall walked outside to check Arlo's work barn for a tarp we could wrap Shane's body in. I said I would get some towels to bunch around his head to keep any more blood from spilling from it, but I sat down at the kitchen table and started getting drunk. Randy Jessup's face was still seared upon my eyeballs, and if I closed them at all, the heavenly light he filled the living room with blazed upon the back of my lids. I poured one double shot of bourbon after another and knocked them back as if I were participating in a drinking competition, and soon enough, my vision got blurry, and the preacher's face blended in with the fuzz.

I drank myself through a half-bottle before Marshall came back inside, and when he found me sitting at the table, he took a seat across from me. My brother watched me fill my glass with a pour that reached its rim and then spilled the brown liquor on the table when I lifted it to my lips. Enough whiskey circulated through my system so that composure became a second thought to me, allowing me to ignore Marshall's scowl without fear of him judging me. I drank until tears streamed from my eyes the way they do when a man sobs from heartbreak.

Marshall sucked in a harsh breath of air until his chest expanded beneath the shirt he wore, and when he let it out, he did it slowly, and I could see him gathering thoughts in his eyes. When he spoke, I thought he would lecture me about my drinking, but instead, he said, "You know Arlo's still got the Trans Am he drove when we was little?"

I fingered the rim of my glass, memories beaming through my drunken fog. "Used to tell us it was the same one Burt Reynolds drove in *Smokey and the Bandit*."

"How many times did he come over and make us watch that movie?"

"Until Mama finally hid that VCR tape."

Marshall smirked. "They got in a knock-down-drag-out about that one."

"It was the only copy of the movie Uncle Arlo owned."

"Hey," Marshall sat up in his chair, his voice rising in volume, "you remember how he used to take us riding in the Trans Am, playing *Midnight Rider* on repeat?"

"It was on cassette, so he had to rewind the tape every time the song ended." I laughed. "He got a bad custom job done, and it'd eat the tape after about five or six plays."

"He'd go and buy a new cassette every time."

I nodded. "He would."

"Mama always told him not to drive like he was Burt Reynolds."

"And Arlo would get us up to a hundred every time."

Marshall smiled, memories gleaming in his eyes. "I remember you crying the first time he ever got us going that fast."

"I didn't cry."

"You thought Arlo was gone wreck us."

"You went and told Mama after he told us not to say nothing."

"She ripped Deddy's ass a new one like he was the one behind the wheel."

"Deddy thought it was the funniest thing," I said, then, "I doubt that car even runs anymore."

Marshall leaned back in his chair until the front legs lifted off the floor, crossed his arms over his chest, raised his eyes to the ceiling, and left them there until our reminiscing dissolved from them. "You're slurring your words, Coy."

"I ain't slurred my words a bit," I said, reaching for my glass and then shoving it away.

"You been slurring 'em the whole time."

"You getting mad at me for having a drink, Marshall?" I asked, my tone slicing from me. "Sorry, I ain't so used to killing; I can't do it without it messing up my nerves."

"It ain't the drinking that's the problem." Marshall let his chair back down, the scowl back from wherever he hid it. "It's the fact that you sat here and drank until you're damn useless to me."

"I ain't useless," I said, shoving my chair back from the table, but when I tried standing, my brain went topsy-turvy, and the floor couldn't support me. I sat down hard in my chair, almost tipping it over, and avoided meeting Marshall's stare.

Marshall let me simmer in my unease before he spoke again. "You agreed to get your drinking under control to help me get Mama back. You ain't a damn bit tried. Part of that is my fault, and I'm willing to say so. But from here on out, you need to get your shit together. If you're getting this tore up over one dead body, what're you gone do when we got a whole pile of 'em, Coy?" Marshall paused, staring at me through the silence. "I'm fixing to take care of this body by myself. Get your ass some sleep and get straight."

After my brother left the table, I poured myself another drink.

13.

Once the living room was clear, I sat on the couch with an almost empty bottle of bourbon and a glass I'd just topped off. The room smelled like tarnished metal despite us getting the blood cleaned up, but my drunken state made it so I didn't care. I closed my eyes to keep the room from spinning, and when I did, a starry-eyed girl waited for me on the other side of them.

The girl wore a ponytail the way cheerleaders do and smiled so wide it forced her freckles to the edges of her face and tugged on my heart as though I were a boy again, developing my first crush. Her giggles made my ears buzz the way they do when they hear a good song on the radio for the first time and don't want it to stop playing. She stood a short throw from me, but her voice carried like a hard pass when she spoke.

What's your name?

Before I could answer, I found myself changing. My body lost muscle tone and height, and I no longer looked down at the girl, but now we stood eye to eye. When I gathered my voice to speak, I noticed it lost the strength that came with being a man and got replaced with the curiousness of boyhood.

I'm Mack, I said.

Where did you get a name like that?

My Mama named me after my great-granddeddy. His name was Mackenzie, and he fought in World War Two.

Mackenzie's a girl's name.

No, it's not.

Yeah-huh.

Well, it can be a boy's name too.

I don't know no boys named Mackenzie.

Well, now you do. What's your name?

I would not have believed the girl's smile could have gotten any wider, but it stretched even further across her face until I could almost count every tooth in her mouth. It was a pretty smile, and I didn't want to see it disappear.

What do you think it is?

I don't know.

Well, guess.

I don't wanna guess.

You're no fun.

I am too.

I don't think so.

Jessica?

Nope! The girl giggled. *I don't even look like a Jessica.*

What do Jessicas look like?

Not like me. Guess again.

Heather?

Wrong again. The girl giggled louder. *One more guess.*

Melissa?

Strike three! You're out! Her giggles turned to laughter, and she clapped along to it. *You're not a very good guesser.*

I know. Tell me your name now.

Okay, she said, her smile became a smirk, and her

freckles returned to her cheeks. *It's Andrea, but my friends call me Andy. You can call me Andy.*

Andy's a boy's name, I said, mocking her name the way she did mine. It made her laugh, and I liked hearing it.

You're silly, she said, then turned serious. *You know we've met before, Mack?*

What?

We sure have. In another life.

I've never lived another life.

You have. It's the one you'll go back to when you open your eyes.

My eyes are open.

Stop thinking, silly. You're never gonna get it.

Andy stood next to me now and held my hand. Her skin was smooth against mine, and the skin along the back of my arm tingled until it reached my neck, my hair standing on ends. I looked into Andy's eyes for the first time and saw how they twinkled like a pair of stars. It was one of the prettiest sights I'd ever seen.

You ever kissed a girl before?

No. Have you ever kissed a boy?

Wanna be the first boy I ever kiss?

My breath caught in my throat, and my lips got itchy, but not in a way that made me want to scratch them. I couldn't get my answer out quick enough, and Andy's smile started to slip.

I do, I said, forcing the words out. *Yeah, I really do.*

Okay! It's all she said before leaning into me and pressing her lips to mine.

The kiss we shared was no more than a peck, but it made us grow older. Andrea's body developed curves in areas I didn't want to look away from, and mine grew until I almost looked like a man again. She ran cool fingertips over my face, tracing its angles down to my neck, and let her hand come to rest upon my chest. My pecks flexed under her touch, and I squeezed her thigh with a firm hand, her eyes brightening with my strength.

This time we kissed with a passion children can't understand. Our mouths worked in unison, speaking in a language incommunicable by words, giving each other permission to explore. My hands shoved themselves under Andy's shirt, her warm skin setting my palms afire, and I tugged it over her shoulders and head. She kissed me harder now, shoving me onto my back, straddling my waist, and toyed with my belt until she got it unbuckled. We moved together now like a pair of dancers, letting our body language speak for us.

I rolled Andy over, slid between her legs, and stared into eyes aglow with cosmic dust. Our kisses strengthened with the intensity our bodies shared, and her tongue slithered into my mouth, reaching the back of my throat, causing me to gag, but she would not let me pull away. Andy clutched the back of my head, digging her fingernails into my hair and scalp, and trapped me against her lips. Her tongue grew inside my mouth, forcing me to open it wider until I thought my jaw would become unhinged. I struggled against her now, passion no longer fueling me. Instead, a panic so severe possessed my body I pummeled her with open-handed blows. Her grip slipped from my head, allowing me to break apart from her, and when I looked down at the woman I'd just made love to, a copperhead filled her mouth. It struck when I tried pulling away, sinking its fangs into my bottom lip, tearing the flesh away, and showering Andy with my blood.

When I opened my mouth to scream, a strong hand fastened over it, bringing me out of my trance.

14.

Caudell Clark looked at me with lucid eyes, his Black skin blending in with the shadows, and pinned me to the couch with a heavy hand. The bottle of bourbon lay across my lap, and I spilled my glass on the floor, a puddle of brown water spreading over the hardwood. I spoke into Caudell's hand, but my words got stifled by it. He let me go, and I got up off the couch.

Caudell stood head and shoulders taller than me and moved with light feet when I stepped around him. When I left the living room, I flipped the light switch, filled it with a dim shine, and grabbed a towel from under the bathroom cabinet. Caudell sat now, his powerhouse arms crossed over his chest, his eyes shining even brighter in the glow of the living room light. He watched me spread the towel over the drink I spilled and didn't bother speaking to me.

I left the living room again, this time walking down the hallway to Arlo's bedroom to check for Marshall. I opened the door with care, not wanting to disturb my brother if he was sleeping, but I found the bed empty and returned to the living room. Caudell sat still—his eyes hardly moving while he watched me come back into the room and take a seat in the chair Shane occupied a few hours before. Neither of us bothered to break the silence. Instead, a screech owl filled in the blank spaces we left open—it trilled and hooted and produced a song only its mate would enjoy.

When Caudell finally spoke, his mouth produced a husky voice like he were some Memphis soul singer meant to break hearts with tender ballads. "You smell like the bottom of this whiskey bottle, Mack."

"I spilled some bourbon on me when I dropped that glass."

"Naw." Caudell sat the bottle on the floor next to an extra-large mud stomper. "You got that sour smell. The one the boozehounds get when they go on those week-long benders. How much you been drinking?"

"Not enough to be considered no boozehound."

Caudell gave me a capstone grin and said, "Sounds like something a boozehound would say."

"What the hell you doing here, Caudell?"

"I'm here cause that pretty lady you been seeing asked me to come watch your ass."

I sat up in the chair. "Do what now?"

"Listen," Caudell's voice rolled in a sweet baritone, "after all this shit's over with, you need to marry that girl—cause this is the second time she's saved your ass. Most women ain't looking out for they man like that."

"How did Jessa even know how to get in touch with you?"

Caudell shrugged. "That's a woman who got her ways, Mack. You been dating her long enough to know. Hate to see how crafty she can become if you get on her bad side."

"Peanut said he sent you on vacation."

"He did. Sent me on one that was nice as hell."

"Then why're you here?"

"I done told ya. That girl you with asked me to come keep an eye on ya."

"But why do what she asks?"

Caudell shrugged again, harder this time. "Mostly cause I got bored. Got tired of laying on the beach listening to the ocean slap the sand. Don't get me wrong, that shit got me relaxed as a motherfucker, but I owe them white boys for what they done."

"What about Peanut?"

"What about Peanut?"

"He ain't gone be happy you came out of hiding, Caudell. He sent you and my brother off to keep yall from getting in any more trouble with these peckerwoods."

"Man, listen," the sweetness left Caudell's tone and got replaced with a hard edge, "Peanut's my closest friend in the world. Been that way since his deddy adopted me when I was little. Ain't nobody I love more than that fat man, but he can go fuck himself if he thinks I'm sitting on the bench while yall two go to war."

"It's hardly a war, Caudell."

"It is now that I'm here."

I turned when the front door slung open and saw Marshall come in mud-covered and sweaty. He stopped inside the doorway, his hand still gripping the doorknob, and his eyes bounced between me and Caudell. A smile spread across my brother's face, catching his eyes on fire, and he said, "Holy shit. Goddammit, all to hell. What in fuck's name are you doing here, brother man?"

"Mack's old lady said yall needed some help."

Marshall's eyes flicked over to me. He said, "You need to marry that damn girl, Coy. It's the second time she's saved your ass. Naw, wait. Third time."

"Third time?" Caudell asked.

"Hell yeah, it is," Marshall said. "You remember Meatloaf Moody, right? That fat sumbitch came in Mack's trailer shooting the place up like it was the damn O.K. Corral. Would've give my brother a third shitting hole, but Jessa scrambled Meatloaf's brain with a baseball bat."

"Marry that girl," Caudell said to me. "Marry her."

Marshall kicked his boots off next to the welcome mat and shut the front door behind him. He asked, "Where you been, brother?"

"Miami."

"That where Peanut sent you?"

"He knows how I do."

"Shit, I got sent to Pigeon Forge. Fucking trailer trash Babylon up there."

"Where you been at?" Caudell asked Marshall. "Coming in here looking like a pig who's been wallering in mud."

Marshall yanked his shirt off, dropped it on the floor next to his boots, and shimmied out of his jeans. "Had to go dump this ol' boy me and Coy talked with. Told us where they keeping Mama at and didn't need him no more after that."

"Where they got her?"

"Someplace called the church. Wouldn't say no more than that."

"We can find out where it is," Caudell said, crossing his arms back over his chest and gazing off into the distance. "Just let me do the asking from now on."

PART THREE

THE DEVIL'S DOORSTEP

1.

I stood under a scalding shower, the water burning the need for alcohol from me. Andy waited outside the shower curtain, reminding me of the dream Caudell woke me from—the taste of the copperhead fresh in my mouth made my bottom lip throb. I stared into the light above me, allowing the incandescent bulb to blister my pupils, hoping it would rob me of my ability to see. Until now, Andy only came to me in my nightmares, providing my mind a reprieve while being awake. I would rather go blind than have my hallucinations of a dead girlfriend haunt me during the day.

A knock on the bathroom door made me pull my eyes from the light and look toward the door. Shadows floated in my vision, and I rubbed the spots away with my palms. The hinges squealed when Marshall opened the door and stuck his head inside. "What the hell's taking you so long, Coy? The water's gotta be cold by now."

"I'm fixing to get out."

"Well, hurry up then. Caudell's got a place or two he wants to stop 'fore we go looking for them dickweasels."

"All I gotta do is get dressed."

"All right then." Marshall closed the door with a snap.

I turned the water off and stood there air drying while I held my breath, hoping Andy wouldn't still be sitting on the toilet lid when I stepped out of the tub.

After exhaling and spending some time refilling my lungs, I yanked the shower curtain aside, the way I would removing a Band-Aid, and found myself in the bathroom alone. I got the towel hanging from the rod next to the shower, patted dry, and redressed myself in the clothes I'd worn the past few days. I smelled stale body odor on the fabric and opened Arlo's medicine cabinet, looking for some cologne to mask the scent. I borrowed a bottle of Nautica, sprayed myself down, and left the bathroom smelling like fresh-cut apples.

Marshall and Caudell waited on the front porch. Sunshine turned the sky the color of orange peel, and humidity blanketed me when I stepped outside; sweat pearled along my forehead and my shirt clung to my arms and back. My brother cut a conversation short and changed the subject to Caudell's '76 Cutlass. It sat next to my pick-up—a cobalt blue paint job glimmered in the morning light with its racing stripes popping in the sunshine.

"It's like I done told you, Caudell, we go riding around in that car of yours, and they'll hear us coming from damn Blackwood."

"Can't all three of us squeeze in your brother's truck."

"The hell you say?" Marshall said, his eyes growing round. "I'll have you know me and Coy fit in there with the Lawson sisters squeezed between us. That cab wasn't near as damn tight as Kayla Lawson neither."

Caudell shook his head. "I ain't leaving my car here for some hillbilly to jack."

"It won't get jacked. Not if we park it in the barn out

back." Marshall flung a thumb over his shoulder, pumping it to add emphasis to his words. "Tell him, Coy."

"Our Uncle Arlo keeps his Trans Am parked back there," I said. "Thing's gathering dust it ain't got touched in so long. Your car'll be fine."

Caudell eyed me, giving me a glimpse into the sorts of consequences we would suffer if he found even the slightest ding on his car. I turned from him, walked over to my truck to escape his glare, opened my door, and got the cell phone from the cupholder. I flipped it open and saw eight missed calls, all of them from Monty. He left a voicemail after his last call, and I punched the code in to hear it.

Monty's voice blasted from the phone's tiny speaker, filling my ear with a blend of fear and anger and dread. "Mack, I know everything you got going on right now," he said. "Peanut talked to me, all right? Told me everything that's going on. Now you need to call me right now, goddammit. There's something you gotta know."

After his message ended, I checked the call log to see how long ago Monty called and, from the time, figured it must have been while I was in the shower. I hit redial, not wanting to avoid him more than I already had. A thread of angst weaved its way through my thoughts, and my heartbeat became a pounding fist inside my chest, my throat swelling with each violent thump.

Monty answered on the second ring, speaking immediately, without saying hello. "Get your ass over to Peanut's now. Right now, you hear me? That gang you and your brother are after hit Peanut's during the night sometime. I don't know who all's hurt or what the hell's going on, but I know you had Jessa staying there and—"

Before Monty could say another word, I snapped my phone shut and slung myself behind the wheel of the truck. My keys weren't in the ignition, and I scrambled, trying to find them. I fished them out of a pocket, couldn't slide them in for my shaking hand, and fumbled them to the floor. Marshall filled the driver's side window and pounded the meat of his fist against it, wanting to know what the hell was going on. Caudell strolled over to the passenger's side, opened the door, and reached across the cab, plucking my keys from the floor.

"Gimme them fucking keys before I smash your fucking face in." I thrust my hand into the side pocket of the door, my hands sweaty and too slick to clasp the thumper's handle.

Caudell cocked his head to the side, his eyes too relaxed to care about my threat. "You need to take a deep breath and drop whatever that is you're reaching for."

Marshall finally got the smarts to open my door, shoved my arm inside the truck, and put himself between me and the thumper. "The hell's done got into you, Coy?

I gripped the steering wheel with both hands, blood draining from my knuckles from the strength I used to hold onto it. Words circulated through my mind, buzzing around too fast for me to grasp any one of them and communicate what Monty told me. Marshall shook me, trying to joggle some sense into me and shake my thoughts loose.

It was Caudell who finally got me to speak. He slid his large frame into the seat next to me, the truck leaning to one side from the added weight, and said, "Listen to me, Mack. I can't hurt whoever needs hurting if you don't calm yourself down and tell me what you just got done hearing on that phone."

I dropped my forehead onto the steering wheel, resting it there until I caught my breath, and when I turned my head to Caudell, his eyes glared down at me with a fierceness shining so bright it hurt to look at. My voice came out strangled when I spoke, "That was Monty. Said something happened at Peanut's, and we need to get over there right now."

2.

Marshall shoved me over to the bitch seat and drove my truck as though we were getting chased by the law. He passed an old lady driving a Grand Marquis on a double yellow line and yanked the truck onto the shoulder when a weather-worn pickup came flying over a hill. He slung chunks of blacktop, getting back onto the road, and spun the wheel hand over hand to make it around a dog-eared turn. The truck's rear end fish-tailed, and the engine rattled from the speeds Marshall got it up to, causing the whole truck to shudder, shaking us all in our seats. Everything outside became a smear as if some artist came along and ran his thumb through the paint, blending all the colors together, until I saw Albermarle Mountain standing in the center of the action.

I pointed at the blinking radio towers, told Marshall he could slow it down, and watched the speedometer drop until it reached a reasonable speed. Tension filled the cab, and we all stiffened, the muscles in our backs and arms flexing so that we all sat up straight and tall. The truck moved almost too slow now, the scenery outside vivid in the morning light. Marshall steered onto Peanut's dirt road and let the pickup cruise along. The property looked undisturbed until we reached the front gate—it had got torn from its track, laid in a ditch off the road, and was now a mangled piece of metal.

My breath caught when I saw a cloud of black smoke swirling over the treetops, and I elbowed my brother to speed it up. Marshall shoved me into Caudell, who leaned forward and told us both to cut the shit before we got him even more pissed off. We rode the rest of the way in silence, listening to the tires crunch gravel, and saw Peanut sitting on his front porch when we reached the house. He boosted himself out of his rocking chair when he saw my truck coming up the driveway, walked to one of the porch banisters, rested his elbows on it, and spat a rope of brown juice in Katie's azaleas.

Marshall parked the truck next to what had been a white cargo van where black smoke now coiled from the smashed-out windows and a low fire broiled inside. A charred body sat behind the wheel, its mouth stretched back, exposing a full set of pearly whites, and its empty sockets stared into the ether. I leaned around Caudell to get a better look at the carnage, but he opened his door, got out of the truck, and his wide back blocked my view.

I scooted across the bench seat, following Caudell out-side, and slid into the stench of cooking bodies—it smelled worse than when Deddy used to gather up all the trash on our property and burn it until nothing but ashes were leftover. I covered my mouth and nose with the back of an arm, but the taste of the driver's simmering meat caught in the back of my throat and got my stomach agitated. The sight of its grilled skin turned my insides over, and I stepped around Caudell before I puked up what little food was on my stomach.

Peanut's laughter got my attention. He didn't stop until

he got red in the face and pounded his chest for air. His words came out wheezy, and he acted the way a little child does when they find something funny an adult doesn't have the imagination to understand. When he could finally speak, he said, "I hope to hell yall ain't here to save my ass because yall are just a little too late."

"What the hell happened?" Marshall said. "Looks like the damn thing got blew up with a bazooka."

Peanut erupted into another round of laughter, jabbed a finger at my brother's words, and said, "Close enough."

"Goddamn."

"Should've heard them boys screaming for their mamas," Peanut said, the humor gone from his voice and turned menacing. "It was downright pathetic. Would've had me feeling sorry for 'em if they hadn't come busting onto my property the way they did. I blew them bastards straight to the Devil's doorstep."

"Goddamn," my brother echoed himself, leaned back against the truck, and kicked a boot toe in the dirt.

"Good thing yall are here, though." Peanut moved away from the railing, walked over to the front porch steps, and came down to us. "Yall can help me get rid of all this 'fore Darryl Tracy gets out here. Told him there ain't a thing to worry about, but he said he's getting calls of an explosion and wants to get out of the office. It'll be hell explaining a blown-up van to him."

Caudell left my side, walked up to Peanut, and they embraced one another with the kind of ferocity team-mates share after clinching a come-from-behind victory. When Peanut pulled away, he snatched off his Georgia Bulldogs trucker cap, swiped the back of an arm across his forehead, and smeared sweat across his brow. The men-acing tone he'd spoken with earlier was gone now and got replaced with the care I only ever heard him use when he spoke of his family. "What the hell are you doing here?"

"Came up here to help," Caudell answered, his smooth voice calm despite Peanut's underlying agitation.

"Ain't nobody called you for help." Peanut's eyes flicked between me and my brother. "Told you to keep your head low until I got this shit flushed."

"You ain't gotta eye them boys cause neither one of them called me."

"Then who the hell did?" Peanut set his narrow eyes back on Caudell.

Caudell turned at the hips and pointed at me. "It was that one's girlfriend."

Peanut stepped around Caudell, took a step toward me, and slapped his hat against his thigh. "That girl's been a pain in my ass from the moment you stuck her with me. Got Katie on her side, and that's a whole bitch I hate having to deal with. I wanna get this gang took care of just so I can get her outta my goddamn house."

"Where is she?"

"She's all right."

"Where is she, Peanut?"

"I said, she's all right."

"Don't fuck with me right now," I said, my voice coming out hard.

"Hey," Peanut said, planting his boots in the dirt. "Watch how you speak to me. This is the second time in so many days you've come onto my property showing me disrespect. Katie took that girl under my care, and I'm making sure she's all right. You ain't got nothing to worry about, but I ain't telling you where she's at."

"If she loses a single hair on her head—"

"Don't make no threats you'll have to see through, Mack."

"Hey, Coy," Marshall came up behind me, put his hands on my shoulders, and did his best to massage the tension from them. "If Peanut says he's taking care of Jessa, you know he damn well is. You gotta trust him."

I shrugged Marshall away. "Why not tell me where you're hiding her?"

"For my own family's protection," Peanut said. "I got Deddy to take 'em to a spot we keep secret for situations like this. She's there with Katie and the boys and won't nobody find 'em. You can bet yer ass on that. If anybody does come around that I ain't let Buford know about, he's got orders to yank their dick out their asshole."

I relaxed, leaned into the side of the truck, ran a hand over my face, and dragged my fingers through my beard.

"You good?"

I nodded.

"One word of advice," Peanut said. "Marry that damn girl. They ain't a pain in somebody's ass like that unless they love ya."

3.

Darryl Tracy got out of his black and gold Chevy Tahoe, took a moment to set his Stetson on his head, checked his reflection in the mirror, and moseyed around the vehicle and over to the porch steps the way a cowboy does in a black and white Western. He stopped at the bottom step, rested a boot on it like he may come up, and took his Aviators off his face. Darryl studied the four of us from under the shadow of his hat's brim and kept sniffing at the air.

I sat in a rocking chair next to Peanut, who rocked in such a steady manner it got me sleepy watching him from the corner of my eye. He got a country-long grin on his face, his bottom teeth stained with tobacco juice, and spoke around his dip, "What you know good, Darryl? Yer allergies messing with ya or something? You got yer nose stuck in the air like one of us ripped some ass."

Peanut paused, letting his grin stretch into a smile, his eyes scrunching until they became squints. He looked at me, said, "Was it you, Mack? I remember when we was kids, you would challenge us all to some farting contests and would bust 'em out so hard you'd stain your drawers. You won every time, though. That's for damn sure."

"You done?" Darryl Tracy asked, resting an elbow on the porch rail.

Peanut rocked back, and when his chair came forward, he said, "Hell, I'm just having a good time with yall."

Darryl took his eyes off us, glancing around for something he might be missing. "Yall got a bar-b-que going out back? Smells like burned meat out here."

"Hell yeah, you want some pulled pork? Ol' Marshall Dooley right there has got the damn magic touch when it comes to some pulled pork. Don't compare to Caudell's ribs, though. Trying to get them two to open a restaurant together. It'd put the damn Pig Shaq outta business." Peanut laughed. "No offense to yer brother."

"What you two Dooley boys doing here?"

Darryl Tracy's soft tone turned callous when his questions turned to me and my brother, probably remembering some trouble we caused that he never could pin on us. Marshall kept a steady stare on Darryl from underneath the mess of hair he'd grown out, leaving a stretch of silence for me to fill.

I shrugged, said, "Got a call from Peanut saying Katie and the boys is outta town visiting her family. Just so happens Jessa is off doing the same. Marshall just got back in town from vacation, and we all decided on doing some day drinking. Got some beer in a cooler if you want one, Darryl."

"That's Sheriff Tracy to you," Darryl said before the wind got the chance to whisk my words away.

"Goddamn, Darryl," Peanut said. "Save the bad cop routine for the interrogation room, son. Mack ain't done nothing but offer you a beer."

"I'm on duty."

"That's fine. You can still show him some appreciation

for being hospitable, or . . ." Peanut stretched the word out to its fringes. "You can get the fuck off my property."

Darryl Tracy set his eyes off in the distance, watching the radio towers on Albermarle Mountain's peak blink in the sunshine. His nostrils flared every time he inhaled a lungful of air, and his jaw muscles flexed from grinding his teeth. When he ended the silence he'd slipped into, he did it without looking at Peanut. "You know what calls I got that brought me out here. I'm just doing what the county pays me to do."

Peanut pounced on Darryl's words. "And who pays you better than the county?"

"Fuck it." Darryl's eyes slashed through the air and cut into Peanut. "Let's cut out this fucking song and dance, all right? I know you got a turf war going with the Ghostface Devils. I been getting calls from the GBI telling me they're moving into North Georgia, and it might solve their problem if the two of yall do away with each other, but you listen to me right now, all right? I don't want none of the citizens of this county becoming blowback because of this bullshit. That happens, and any deal we've ever had is off the table. I'll burn this fucking compound to the ground."

"Well, Darryl," Peanut sat up in his rocking chair like a king declaring war on an opposing kingdom, "pray to God that I win this thing because there won't be no deals with the Devils. They'll put one of their fucked up own in yer place."

Darryl sighed, put his Aviators back on, and lingered for a breath or two before turning his back on us and moseying over to the Tahoe. He said over his shoulder, "Yall have a good one."

"You do the same," Peanut said, his voice jovial again. "Sure you don't want to take a plate with ya?"

Darryl slammed the SUV's door without answering, cranked the engine, and backed around my truck without waving.

After the dust his tires stirred up settled, Peanut said to us, "Yall ready to end this fucking war?"

4.

Peanut," I said, getting out of my rocking chair and blocking him from moving, "we ain't doing shit until you tell us what the fuck is going on."

Peanut dropped into his chair, rocked it backward, and knocked into the wall. The commotion got his dog to barking and the animal barreled through the screen door, almost tearing it from the hinges. "Goddammit, Mack, he tears that door up, and I'll let him bite a chunk from yer ass, you hear me?"

The German Shepherd spun in circles at my feet, its tail wagging hard enough to keep it off balance. I reached down and scratched him between the ears until he got calm and laid down on the porch.

"When did you get a dog?" Marshall asked, leaning forward and rubbing its belly. The animal rolled onto its back, tongue hanging out of its mouth, and kicked its paws in the air.

Peanut watched his dog soak up all the loving and shook his head. "Here not too long ago. Katie's done got him pussified, as yall can see."

"Can't never let your woman make friends with your dog," Caudell said. "I told you that before you got him."

"Shit, you sit Katie down and feed her that line of bull-shit." Peanut clicked his tongue, and his dog rolled over and leaped into his lap, licking Peanut about the face. "She treats you better than she does me, doesn't she, Otis? Can't get no pussy for this bed hog right here."

"No wonder the dog got pussified," Caudell said, lean-ing back in his chair, giving Peanut a critical eye.

"Shut the fuck up, Caudell. Don't get me started on that ol' pitbull you used to have. Treated that damn dog better than any woman you ever been with. Acted like it was a durn princess." Peanut snapped his fingers, and Otis hopped back onto the porch and sat, waiting for its next command. "Now what the hell's got you getting all aggres-sive, Mack? I'll need a beer if you keep acting thisaway."

I paced back and forth now, sorting through all my thoughts, unable to pin any down because Andy watched me. She sat on the hood of my truck, patting her bare feet against the bumper, a ghostlike smile curling the corners of her mouth. The thought of a beer wormed its way into my brain, getting me on edge and thirsty. A taste of alco-hol would help even me out, but I wouldn't be able to stop after one can. I'd want to keep the buzz going until I drowned out the whole world.

"Mack, where the hell's yer head at right now, son? Yer getting me nervous walking back and forth like that. Fixing to march a hole in my damn porch."

I stopped pacing and leaned into a porch rail, letting the wood's rough texture scratch some feeling into me. I blinked hard until I couldn't see through the eye floaters, hiding Andy from my sight. After my vision cleared and I saw the spot where she sat moments before was now vacant, I turned to face Peanut and wrangled a question from my frantic brain.

"What got this turf war started? Don't bullshit me neither."

Peanut sighed, ran his pointer finger through his bottom lip, and shoveled his dip out of his mouth. He flung the tobacco into Katie's azaleas and got a can from a front pocket. "I need a fresh fucking dip if we're gone talk about this."

"Gimme one too."

"You can have what's leftover."

Peanut packed the can, slapping the same pointer finger against the lid, then got a pinch out and shoved it into his bottom lip. He passed me the can, and I got what was left. A nicotine rush surged through me, flicking all the right switches in my brain to cool me down. I spat into the yard and let myself float along.

"It's Kendall Murdoch," he said. "That bastard is using that gang to fight me."

"Wait a minute," Marshall said. "We talking about the same guy who used Randy Jessup's church to launder money?"

Peanut nodded. "Same one."

"I thought you said it would yank the rug from under his feet if you got all that money?"

"It did. For a time, anyway. Now he's paired up with the Devils and is trying to make a comeback."

"Why would he get himself tied up with some white supremacists?" I asked.

"Who fucking cares, Mack? Think about where we live. You believe the people whose votes he's trying to win truly care about him letting some racist shitbags do his dirty work?" Peanut spat. "They'll cheer him on Peachtree Street, son."

Peanut wasn't wrong. No matter how much things change over the years, some problems never go away.

I spat into the yard and turned to face Peanut, my arms stretched across the railing. Otis had curled up at his boots and lifted nothing but his eyes when I spoke, "Why them?"

Peanut sighed and hefted himself up straight like answering the question weighed him down. "Because they're fucking brutal," he said, his eyes darkening in the sunshine. "Get yer deddy to tell you some stories about 'em. I know he's had to deal with 'em in Sweetwater. You don't get in that gang unless you've killed a man of color. That ain't no shit."

"I told you how it scared the hell outta Deddy when I told him me and Caudell were dealing with 'em," Marshall said. "Thought he was gone have a panic attack right there in the middle of the prison. Wanted me to get my ass as far from Atlanta as I could. Told me to get a cottage in Derry, Maine, and stay for the summer. What the fuck does Deddy know about Derry, Maine?"

I caught a glimpse of Andy smiling at me from the opposite end of the porch, dropped my eyes to the floorboards, squeezed them shut, and kept them closed until my eyeballs strained from the pressure. When I opened them again, Andy was gone. "Well, what do we do now?"

"Go to war," Peanut said, his voice low and heavy.

"Do we even got enough people to go to war with 'em, Peanut? There ain't nothing but the four of us here."

"We got me," Caudell said. "When has that never not been enough?"

I shook my head. "We gotta be smarter than that. Where's the men you've had guarding this place?"

Peanut spat into a trash can next to his rocking chair. "I told them bastards to take a hike after they let those Devils bust through my damn gate. Watched every single one of 'em get trigger scared. They didn't know what the fuck to do. If Katie didn't have some presence of mind about her, we'd all be maggot food right now."

"So it's just the four of us then?"

Peanut shrugged. "Want me to call a temp service?"

I lifted my eyes from the floor, locking them onto Peanut's, and said, "No. Not with what I plan on us doing."

5.

Peanut leaned back in his rocking chair, knocking it into the wall, got a woof from a napping Otis, and hid his face behind a hairy paw. He looked at me from between his fingers and couldn't speak for my brother raising hell.

"Where the fuck did you get a dumbass idea like this, Coy?" Marshall said, flinging his arms all around, almost slapping Caudell. "I mean, goddamn, I know I've come up with some stupid shit over the years, but it ain't never been nothing that could get us killed."

"Stealing money from that church almost got me killed, Marshall."

Marshall threw up both hands, patting them in the air, hushing me down. "I ain't never come up with nothing that would get us killed intentionally, but this right here," he pointed at me, "will most certainly get us killed."

"It ain't a bad idea," I said.

"It ain't a good one either," Caudell replied, resting his chin on a pair of balled fists. "We fuck up even just a little bit, and it'll be like your brother says. Dead as a motherfucker."

"Either one of yall got anything better?"

"They don't," Peanut said, leaning forward, taking his ball cap from his head, and spitting into the yard. "It's the first damn idea I've heard that I think is half reasonable."

"You got to be fucking kidding," Marshall said, staring bullet holes through Peanut. "How many other ways can I say this is a dumbass idea?"

"Dumbass idea or not, it's the best option on the table."

"Nope." Marshall shook his head. "You're too close to this to be making any decisions."

"The hell I am," Peanut said, raring up.

"Marshall," I said, speaking over Peanut. "It's all about getting Mama back. Think about that. We got to be smarter than the Devils are here because they're the ones who got all the power."

"Listen to yourself, Coy. There ain't nothing smart about kidnapping Kendall Murdoch. We get our assess arrested, and we won't be doing Mama no good."

"Won't do her no good if we end up dead at the hands of the Devils either."

"You not think it's a very real possibility that we'll end up dead at the hands of Kendall Murdoch too?"

"Shit," Peanut spat. "Kendall Murdoch ain't never had a speck of blood on his hands. Bet the man ain't never even had bug juice on the sole of his boots. Probably gets his wife to smash 'em for him."

Marshall turned to Peanut and spoke in a biting tone. "You not think he ain't got men watching his back?"

"Marshall Dooley, you better watch how you speak to me, son. I'll send yer ass back to Pigeon Forge and not think a second thought about it."

"I'll fucking go on my own. Tell me I won't."

It got quiet on the porch except for the Carolina Wrens singing their morning songs, but Marshall and Peanut maintained such a blistering stare even Vaseline wouldn't moisten their scabbiness.

Caudell got out of his chair, came to stand next to me, and stared out at the yard. "I got something to say once yall get done with this playground shit." He turned to face everybody, leaned his weight into the porch railing, and waited for Peanut and my brother to break the grip their eyes wrestled over.

Once they looked at him, he said, "There ain't no good ideas here. We can either do like Mack says and use Kendall Murdoch to bargain with the Devils, or we can go straight at 'em and bust some fucking heads. The consequences are shitty no matter what we do. Let's put it to a fucking vote instead of pissing on each other's morning."

"I vote for the head-busting," Marshall said, throwing a hand in the air.

"We know where my vote goes," I said.

"I'm with Marshall on this one," Caudell said, adding his vote to the conversation.

We all turned our eyes on Peanut, who ran a tongue over his lips, and spat a streak of tobacco juice into the trash can next to him. "Mack's got my vote."

"This shit didn't get us nowhere," Marshall said, dropping his hand in his lap.

"Naw, it did," Peanut said. "I got the winning vote."

"What do you mean?"

"Well, seeing as how I'm the boss here, my vote counts for two," Peanut said, getting out of his chair with Otis following him. "Now yall bring yer asses on, and let's go hunt us a Kendall."

6.

After Peanut made some phone calls, we all loaded into his Bronco. Otis got in the backseat with me and Marshall, sat between us, and caught sight of a squirrel running through the yard. His eyes followed the tree rat and the muscles in his legs flexed like he might lunge through the windshield and chase after it. I laced my fingers through the German Shepherd's collar in case he got hungry, but Peanut turned to face us, snapped his fingers, and pointed at Otis. The dog's eyes lost focus, and he leaned forward to sniff Peanut's fingertip.

Peanut scratched the dog between the ears, glanced down at the thumper leaning against the seat between my legs, and said, "You plan on busting some kneecaps with that thing?"

"Shit," Marshal said. "You ort to have seen how he busted the ol' boy we interrogated in the shin with that bastard. Hurt him so bad it made me wanna cry."

Peanut whistled and shook his head. "Goddamn, Mack, some countries would consider that a form of torture."

"Got me the information I wanted out of him."

"What's that?"

"Where they're keeping Mama."

"Yeah," Marshall said. "He said they got her at someplace called the church but wouldn't say where it is. Got any ideas on that?"

"Nope." Peanut turned back to the steering wheel and cranked the truck. He looked at us in the rearview mirror. "This is why kidnapping Kendall Murdoch is our best bet. Yer Mama ain't got time for us to figure out shit like that."

Marshall leaned forward, propping an arm on the back of Peanut's seat. "One thing I'm wondering here, what if they don't go for an exchange? We could end up taking the man hostage, and it not do us no good."

Peanut didn't answer. He got a notebook of CDs out, flipped through the pages until he found the disc he wanted, and fed it to the stereo. The crisp sound of a fiddle played through the speakers, and Travis Tritt sang about a country club. Peanut shifted into drive and answered my brother. "The thing about the Ghostface Devils is they don't exist outside of Sweetwater without Kendall Murdoch's support. We threaten his safety, and it threatens their gang's very existence."

"Then how does it benefit you to bargain with 'em?"

Peanut waited for traffic to pass and steered onto the road, heading toward the highway. "Because part of the deal is gone be for Kendall to keep 'em outta Tugalo County. They'll have to crawl back into Sweetwater without access to this place."

Marshall nodded, understanding the scope of what Peanut hoped to accomplish, sat back in his seat, and scratched the dog's neck. Otis leaned his head close to my brother, got right up in his face, and gave him puppy kisses in return.

"Okay," he said in between them. "Now tell me why Kendall Murdoch will go for that?"

Peanut didn't hesitate to answer. "Because if he don't, I'll cut his pecker off and feed it to him."

After Peanut got us on the highway, driving north toward Rabun County, and Travis Tritt started singing about putting some drive in his country, I decided to ask some questions of my own. "Who were you talking on the phone with, Peanut?"

Peanut laughed the way a middle schooler does when they have a secret the rest of their friends don't know about, turned up the stereo's volume, and said over the music, "I love this part right here." Peanut drummed an offbeat rhythm on the steering wheel and bobbed his head along to a harmonica solo, sang off-key, and played air guitar, letting the Bronco drift into the opposite lane. Caudell reached a hand over and kept the truck from colliding with oncoming traffic.

I let him have his fun, and when the song faded into a ballad, I asked, "You done now?"

"I swear yall ain't got good taste in music," he said, adjusting the volume so we didn't have to raise our voices. "I was on the phone with this ol' boy who works for me. He's got a job with Kendall and was letting me know his whereabouts."

"How did you manage to get somebody working for Kendall on your payroll?"

"Almost everybody is capable of getting bought, Mack, so I always outbid the competition."

"What about the ones who can't get bought?"

Peanut found me in the rearview mirror. "I shoot 'em. Can't trust a man who ain't willing to play ball."

Signs advertising Tallulah Gorge started popping up along the roadside, and the mountains got taller now that we were among some of the highest summits in Georgia. We exited the highway, driving toward one of the lakes now.

"Don't know why you ain't shot me yet," I said, speaking more out of mockery than any real concern.

Peanut snorted. "Don't think it ain't crossed my mind. But I ain't shooting my family. No matter how bad some of yall might piss me off."

We didn't speak for the remainder of the drive. I leaned forward and propped an arm on the back of Caudell's seat. Otis stuck his head right next to mine and licked my face while I studied the route Peanut drove. The houses got fancier and more affluent the closer we got to the lake, with cars costing more than the doublewide I rented parked in the driveways.

Peanut steered onto a road sloping down into the woods and came to a two-story cabin built from chestnut logs with a double-decker front porch. I recognized Kendall Murdoch's tricked-out Chevy Silverado with all-terrain tires, a brush guard on the front, and a light bar across the roof. It wasn't a luxury vehicle like the cars parked next to it but probably cost as much. Peanut parked the Bronco crossways, blocking the only way people could leave.

Marshall got up next to me, said, "Looks like Kendall's having himself a party."

"Sure looks that way, don't it, boys?" Peanut said. "Wonder how pissed he gets for us crashing it?"

"We're just gone take him in front everybody?" I asked.

"Hell, why not?" Peanut shrugged. "We might not get no other chance."

"You don't think it'll be smarter to take him when no one else ain't around?"

"Ain't none of these people gone say shit. Trust me on that."

"What do you mean?"

"Just wait and see, Mack." Peanut reached across the Bronco, opened the glove compartment, and got out an old Polaroid camera. "Marshall, you got the knife I gave you?"

"Carrying it in my pocket."

"Good. You and Caudell slash all these tires and then meet me and Mack inside."

7.

Peanut whistled when he got out of the Bronco, and Otis hopped over the front seat, following him out. "Grab your knocker there, Mack. Let's go say hello."

I came around the back end of the Bronco and followed Peanut toward the cabin. Caudell and my brother were already slicing long gashes into the sidewall of the tires, flattening them to the rims.

Otis walked next to Peanut, and I lagged a few steps behind. We stopped at the front porch, where Peanut turned to me, placed a finger over his lips, and whispered, "Let me do all the talking when we get inside, all right? If I need you to do anything other than look mean, I'll say so. Shouldn't nobody cause us any real trouble, but Otis will take care of 'em if they do."

Otis cocked his head at the mention of his name, and Peanut ascended the front porch steps. He tiptoed toward the door, careful not to set his full weight down on the boards and stopped at the welcome mat. He turned to see what I waited on, and I took the same path he did with Otis a step or two behind me, his nails clicking on the wood.

When we reached the door, Peanut placed a hand on the knob—the Polaroid dangling from his wrist—and crossed a finger over his lips once more. He twisted the handle, and we walked in on one hell of a sight. I wanted to tear my eyes away but couldn't do so for the shock of having never seen such a thing.

A man who looked as though he were the product of a rhinoceros humping a pug had Kendall Murdoch bent over the arm of a couch, pounding away at his backdoor the way a SWAT officer does when barging into a trap house. A gorgeous woman with an angular face, cat-like eyes, pouty lips, and top-dollar knockers—who I'd only ever seen in Kendall's campaign ads—lay spread eagle on the couch, grinding her Brillo Pad in her husband's face, drowning in waves of pleasure.

Naked bodies surrounded them, engaging in various sex acts, some I'd only ever seen in movies Deddy had kept stashed in an antique trunk under his and Mama's bed. Men slobbered all over each other and shoved their faces between thighs regardless of what sort of luggage folks carried. The women didn't act much different, twisting their legs around whatever body they could clamp onto, creating a naughty kind of Twister.

Not a single one of them was aware of our presence until Peanut slammed the door. A collective gasp escaped the orgy, and every face turned to see who barged in. Peanut smiled like this was nothing out of the ordinary, lifted the camera to an eye, pressed the shutter, and everyone hid their faces except for Kendall Murdoch. He peeled his face from between his wife's thighs and came around the couch with his hulking lover following a few steps behind.

"What you know good, Kendall?" Peanut said, still snapping pictures.

Kendall's body glistened in the room's natural light, his stomach muscles flexing from the way he stood and squinted at us from the flash going off in his eyes. His mouth made a jagged line across his face and his voice cut when he spoke. "Kill him, Terrence. Kill him right here and now."

Peanut whistled before Terrence could get moving, and Otis filled the room with barking—the hackles on the back of his neck stood stiffer than Kendall's pecker, and he bared his teeth in case either one of them wanted to try their luck. Neither man moved except to take a few steps backward, their faces overcome with apprehension now, which made Peanut laugh.

Marshall came into the cabin about this time, stopping dead in the middle of the doorway, and Caudell barreled right into him. The both of them stumbled forward, almost tumbling into me, but I caught my brother with an arm, and Caudell regained his balance. Marshall glared all around the room, his eyes torn between enjoying the sight of naked women and avoiding catching a gaze of a hard pecker.

"Good Godamighty," Marshall said. "How do I get invited to one of these?"

"This ain't your kinda party, Marshall," Peanut said.

"It sure as hell could be."

"Not if you don't like playing on both sides of the fence."

"Do what?"

Peanut left my brother's question unanswered and said, "Marshall, you and Caudell gather up everybody's things and bring me all the cell phones yall find. Ain't nobody gone be needing 'em from here on out." A few of the ladies sniffed back tears, but Peanut ignored them, speaking to me instead, "Mack, take that thumper of yers and smash all the landlines, please. I'd hate for anybody to make an unnecessary phone call."

I moved quickly, swinging the thumper overhead, smashing it down on a telephone sitting on a glass end table. Glass shattered, sprinkling all over the hardwood floor, and the phone busted into pieces, its ringer trilling one final time before warbling into nothing. Ladies cried now, and the men who surrounded them did their best to give comfort without it becoming sexual. Peanut laughed, making the moment all the more awkward, and I left the room looking for more telephones.

I found them in the kitchen, guest rooms, upstairs in a game room, one in the master bedroom, and found a cordless telephone hanging in the master bath. I smashed them each with the hitch-end of the thumper, blasting them all over the rooms they occupied, leaving them inoperable, and came back to the living room to find everyone dressed and gathered in a corner. Nobody cried now but listened to Peanut, fear all over their expressions.

"Yall do everything I just said and won't nothing come of these pictures I took. They'll stay locked up in a safe I got and won't never leave it, understand?"

Nobody answered.

"I asked yall a question."

"We understand," a man said, his voice quavering.

Marshall and Caudell came back into the room, carrying a grocery bag full of phones with them, and tossed it at Peanut's feet.

"That's all we could find," Marshall said.

"We'll take 'em with us. You ready, Kendall?"

A woman spoke now, her voice high-pitched and hysterical. "Please don't hurt him."

Peanut's eyes flicked over the faces until he found Kendall's wife. Her cat-like eyes were bloodshot from crying, and she mashed those pouty lips together in a flat line.

He smiled at her and said, "As long as Kendall is willing to bargain with me, I won't harm a single hair on his head."

"Please," she said once more, trailing off into tears, and hid her face in the rhino's chest.

"I'll be fine, Amelia," Kendall said, sounding braver than he looked. "Peanut knows what will happen if I'm hurt."

Amelia turned to speak, but we left before she could say a word.

8.

I opened the back of the Bronco to drag Kendall out but got startled when I saw Andy sitting cross-legged next to him, staring at me. Her mouth tightened until her lips lost all color, and her eyes filled with a forlornness one can only know when they lay sleepless in a bed with a lover they have no desire to share their space with. Chills curled the hairs on the back of my neck, and I shivered from the sensation of cold water running down my spine, and I became aware of the thirst I'd ignored since leaving Arlo's cabin. My mouth watered from the thought of having a drink, and my belly yearned for the warmth a swallow would bring.

Marshall elbowed me out of the way, and Andy disappeared at his intrusion. "The hell you standing here waiting on, Coy? Acting like you seen a damn ghost or something."

We'd duct-taped a pillowcase over Kendall's head, cut a nose-sized hole in it for him to breathe through, and taped his wrists together to keep him from fighting or trying to get loose. Marshall guided him out of the back of the truck, and I stepped out of the way, still looking for

Andy to reappear and let me know what I'd done to make her so unhappy.

Peanut stood at the top of the front porch steps, Otis laying on the floorboards next to his boots, and asked, "Yall bringing him in here or not? I can feel myself getting older with all the loafering yall doing."

"We're coming," Marshall hollered, dragging Kendall along.

I reached for the Bronco's hatch and hesitated, giving Andy another opportunity to appear, but when my arm started tingling from getting held over my head, I slammed the door shut and turned to see Peanut staring down at me.

"What's got you acting all peculiar, Mack?" He asked, cocking his head at an angle like it would give him some special insight into my behavior.

I came up the front porch steps and stopped on the one below Peanut because he blocked my way. He focused a sharp stare on me, and the weight of it weakened my knees, causing me to reach for the porch railing for added support. We stood there, neither of us speaking, listening to the leaves rustle in the walnut trees. His big belly expanded until his chest got tight, and when he exhaled, a gust of air blew over me like a summer storm was blowing down from the mountains. A grin formed at the corners of Peanut's mouth, and he clapped me on the shoulder and said, "I forget what kinda weirdo you can be sometimes."

Peanut said no more, turned to go inside the house and clicked his tongue for Otis to come. I followed the dog into the living room, where Kendall sat alone on a leather sofa and Marshall reclined in a chair next to him. Caudell stood behind the couch, his fists buried in the leather cushions, looking down at Kendall despite the man being unable to see who loomed above him. Peanut took a seat on a cedar coffee table and pointed an index finger at the spot next to Kendall, and Otis hopped onto the couch. Caudell reached for the opening allowing Kendall to breathe and tore a hole big enough for his head to fit through.

Kendall's eyes widened at the sight of Peanut sitting in front of him and began pulsing with fear after Peanut whistled and Otis started growling inches from Kendall's face.

Peanut looked over at me, a smile stretching from ear to ear, and then shared it with Caudell and Marshall before letting Kendall see it. "You wouldn't think a dog named after Otis Redding could be so damn scary, would ya? My wife wanted to name him that because Otis Redding is her favorite singer. She gets whatever she wants, and that name is unassuming anyway. Hell, the dog hardly looks scary, and half the time doesn't even act it, but let me whistle one more time, and he'll tear your fucking head from yer shoulders."

"Peanut—"

"Don't bother speaking, Kendall. Hearing your voice will just piss me off, and I will let this dog tear into ya. He ain't eat in a day and a half and is damn hungry. Look at all the drool. He'll enjoy snacking on that pretty face of yers."

Peanut paused, waiting for Kendall to speak, but he stayed quiet, except for the heavy breathing and whimpering he tried to force back.

"There ain't much I want out of ya, and I'll let ya go unharmed if you do everything I say." Peanut waited, said, "This is the part where you ask me what I want."

"What—" Kendall started but couldn't finish for panic catching his tongue. He glanced at Otis from the corners of his eyes, and when the dog didn't snap, he went on, "What is it you want, Peanut?"

"I hate how you say my name. Drawing it out like that sounds so prissy."

"Sorry?"

"Shut up and listen."

Kendall nodded.

"You've caused me and my friends here some problems you need to solve. Those rimjobs you got doing yer dirty work are hellbent on killing my best friend there because of his skin color, and they took Mack and Marshall's mama. You ain't ever met Rhonda Dooley, but that's the goodest woman you'll ever meet and, I swear to God, if I find out a single hair on her head has been harmed, I'm gone snatch up Amelia and do to her whatever was done to Rhonda."

"Hey, now," Kendall said, leaning forward, "you keep whatever this bullshit is between—"

Peanut whistled, and Otis lunged into Kendall, knocking him onto his side, so his face got buried in throw pillows and made him yell for Peanut to command the dog to stop. Otis loomed over Kendall, his paws planted in the cushions on either side of him, and leered down at him, drool dangling from the corners of his mouth, waiting for Peanut to whistle again.

Peanut scratched Otis behind the ear, the show of affection not even breaking the dog's concentration, and said, "If you wanted this bullshit to stay between us, you should've thought about that before I had to go and put my family in hiding, Kendall. Those peckerwoods showed up here intending to harm my wife and boys. Would've done it, too, but I blew those bastards straight up Satan's ass crack."

"I never meant to get your family involved."

"Well, they are."

"I'm sorry."

Peanut sat up, his back stiff and shoulders tight. "The fuck you say? You're sorry? They make an attempt on my family's life, and you're sorry? Listen, ya sumbitch, I still got the van around back with their charred corpses in it, keep talking some stupid shit like that, and I'll make yer ass spend the night out there."

Kendall shook his head, and a pillow fell over on him from all the shaking. He said from under it, "What do you want me to do, Peanut? I'll do everything I can to make this right with you."

Peanut whistled, and Otis relaxed, sitting back on his haunches. Caudell reached down, took Kendall by the shoulders, sat him upright, and held him in place. Kendall's hair lay lopsided and messy now from the way he lay on the couch, his eyes were bloodshot with panic, and snot ran down from his nose and around his lips. The perfect image he presented in his campaign commercials got shattered, and Peanut commented on it, "Goddamn, I wish I'd brought that camera inside so I could get a picture of yer face. Wouldn't nobody vote for such a pathetic-looking little bitch."

Kendall squeezed his eyes shut, wrinkling the corners of his face, and inhaled deep breaths of oxygen, holding it until it all blew out his nostrils. "Peanut, tell me what it is I can do to make all this right."

"I'm disappointed you even have to ask."

"Just tell me, goddammit."

Peanut backhanded Kendall, snapping his head to the side, and he would've fallen over if not for Caudell holding him in place. "Watch yer tone with me, boy. You ain't fixing to talk to me like I'm the shit you wipe off your boots."

"Tell me what you want me to do, and I'll make it

happen," Kendall said, forcing the words out between clenched teeth.

Peanut stretched his back and rubbed his belly, leaned back over, rested his elbows on his knees, and said, "Well, if we're gone get down to business, here's what I want. First, you're gone arrange a meetup with the Ghostface Devils. Tell 'em to bring Rhonda Dooley for an exchange. We'll take her, and they can have you. If that goes off without a hitch, and she tells me not a hair on her head's been mussed outta place, I'll let yall go without letting Caudell fulfill whatever violent fuckery he's imagining. Sorry, Caudell."

Caudell nodded.

Peanut went on, "Second, the Ghostface Devils ain't to step foot in Tugalo County from here on out. If word gets to me that they crossed a toe over the county line, then I'll sic Otis on you and, boy, it won't be to tease you next time. I'll let that dog fucking feast, understand?"

"Understood," Kendall said without arguing.

"Well, shit," Peanut said, smiling big. "Who says you ain't willing to negotiate, Kendall? Maybe you oughta be in office. We could get along real good."

"This is the only deal you and me are ever going to make."

"I've heard that shit before." Peanut turned to my brother, said, "Pass me that phone there, Marshall. Kendall's got a call to make."

9.

Peanut dialed the number Kendall recited to him and turned the speakerphone on, so we could all hear his conversation. It only rang once before the call got answered, and the voice which came over the line put me back in my bedroom from a few nights before, where the skinhead stood before me, aiming a gun at the center of my chest, and threatened to let Ichabod do whatever harm he could conceive of to Jessa.

"Hello," Meyer said.

"Hey, Meyer," Kendall said, adding a friendliness to his tone that hadn't been there a few moments before. "It's Kendall."

"Why are you calling me from an unlisted number?"

"I got some important business I need to talk to you about."

"Then you know I don't talk business over the phone."

"Well," Kendall paused, leaning in closer to the telephone, "this is an extenuating circumstance, and you're going to have to make an exception."

"No exceptions," Meyer said, his voice cold. "You wanna talk business, then bring yer ass over here."

"I'm not in a position to do that, Meyer."

"Then come over when you are."

"You're not listening to me."

"I'm hearing every word you're saying, and you ain't done nothing but bullshit with me, and I'm getting tired of it, so I'm hanging up now. Come over when you wanna talk."

"Don't hang up," Kendall said, panic rising in his voice.

"You better listen to him," Peanut added. "It'll get real ugly for him if you end this telephone call, and you know as well as I do, if things get ugly for Kendall Murdoch, they'll get even uglier for the Ghostface Devils."

"Who the hell is this?"

"Don't play dumb, peckerwood. You know who this is."

"The fuck do you want?"

"It's like Kendall said, we got some business to discuss."

"I ain't talking business with you."

"You will if you want Kendall to continue supporting you. I can make that end real quick."

"We both know the only way that ends is by you doing something you ain't got balls big enough to do."

A silence settled in the room, and Peanut's bodyweight sank to his feet. His chubby cheeks went slack, his shoulders slumped, and his fingers loosened their grip on the telephone, but his eyes got hard and turned harsh when Meyer started laughing.

"What's wrong with you, fat boy, can't handle the truth?" Meyer asked, doing a poor Jack Nicholson impression.

Peanut let out a shrill whistle. Otis snarled and bit into Kendall's arm, tearing through skin and hair, and shook his head from side to side the way a wolf does when it has a bunny clenched in its jaws. Kendall screamed and struggled to get his arm back, but Caudell pinned him against the couch cushions, not letting him get away from the dog.

Marshall sat up in his chair, his eyes bright with shock, and my stomach muscles clenched, catching the smell of corroded metal and seeing blood spill on the floor.

"What the fuck?" Meyer yelled on the phone. "What the fuck is going on?"

Peanut laughed, watching Kendall's arm get gnawed on like leftover beef shank.

"Talk to me now, goddammit," Meyer hollered, straining his voice.

Peanut clicked his tongue, and Otis stopped trying to tear Kendall's arm from its socket but didn't unclench his teeth. "Now, I ain't fed this dog in two days, and it can get a whole lot worse than this," Peanut said, too much calm in his voice. "You gimme one reason to, and I'll let him tear Kendall's throat out."

"Do whatever he wants, Meyer," Kendall howled.

"You're fucking crazy," Meyer said. "Who trains a dog to act that way?"

"Has prison done made you soft, boy?"

"Come find out how soft I am."

"Hey, now," Peanut said, laughter in his voice. "You asking me to come make you my yardbitch?"

"Keep making jokes, Peanut."

"All I'm saying is my wife don't like sharing."

"Talk to the dial tone, motherfucker."

"Peanut," I said, getting his attention. "Quit playing games and get Mama back."

"Who's that?" Meyer asked. "That you Mack Dooley?"

"It's me," I answered.

Meyer's breathing filled the telephone speaker, and his voice turned dark when he spoke, "You know that was my cousin Wade whose nose you fucked up? Got the kid laid up cause of how you busted his ribs."

I shrugged at the telephone, said, "Too bad stupid can't get beat outta somebody."

"Let me tell you what was stupid—"

"Save the lectures for whoever gives a fuck," Peanut said. "The last goddamn thing we need is for some white power jackfag trying to teach us a lesson, all right?" Peanut stood from the coffee table and started pacing. "Now, let's move on to the business I called you for."

"You can hang up this telephone right now because I ain't doing business with some motherfucker like you."

"Yeah, I thought you might say that, and it's fine if you wanna refuse what I got to offer, but you need to know what sorta penalty comes with turning me down."

"I don't give a fuck what it is."

"You will when I dump Kendall Murdoch's bloody corpse on the front steps of that place you're calling the church. That's on Highway 17, right? You been squatting in the old casket factory. Must be sleeping in the chapel they had."

"What the fuck?"

Peanut smiled when he caught the darts I stared at him, not caring how it pissed me off knowing he lied to me.

"C'mon, son," he said to Meyer. "You think I don't know what goes on in this town of mine? Got a call from a deputy sheriff the day you moved in. Only reason you got to stay there as long as you have is cause I told them not to kick you out. In retrospect, I should've listened to that deputy. It was a mistake, on my part, to think the best way to keep an eye on my enemies is by keeping them close. Learned my lesson there. I'm serving you an eviction notice right now, though. It's time for you to get the fuck outta my county but not before you give Rhonda Dooley back."

"Yall ain't getting the Dooley bitch back."

Peanut raised a hand when my brother got up from his chair and motioned for him to sit back down. When Marshall obeyed, Peanut answered, "I figured you might say that and I'm gone give you time to think this through because you ain't in no position to bargain with me."

"There ain't nothing for me to think about."

"Kendall would disagree with you."

"Let him disagree then."

"All right," Peanut said and whistled, letting loose the devil which rested inside Otis. The dog sunk its canines deeper into Kendall's arm, razoring through skin and muscle, and squirted blood all over the room. Kendall shrieked from the pain inflicted upon him, thrashing on the couch but unable to tear free because of how Caudell pinned him down.

Peanut ignored Meyer's yelling, holding the telephone close to the action, allowing him to hear Kendall beg.

"Come get this bitch, Peanut! Are you not listening to me? Come get her!"

Peanut clicked his tongue, and Otis froze, his jaws still clenching Kendall's arm and growling from how it riled him up. "I ain't coming to you. You're getting out of that casket factory and meeting me at a place of my choosing."

"I ain't coming out to yer compound."

"I didn't say you were. Besides, I don't allow no jizz nazis to step foot on my property no way. My Mama would roll over in her grave if I did."

"I'll spit on your mama's grave."

Thunderheads formed in Peanut's eyes, but he kept the storm from raging, said, "This is the one and only time I let a comment you make about my mama slide. You ever speak ill of her again, and it'll be you I sic this dog on."

Peanut paused long enough for the threat to sink in and asked, "You know where the old middle school is?"

Meyer spoke through heavy breathing, "I can find it."

"Meet me there in two hours," Peanut said, hung up the phone, and snapped his fingers. Otis let go of Kendall's arm and hopped off the couch, took a seat next to Peanut, and leaned into his leg. Kendall cradled his arm against his chest and sobbed like a small child does after skinning their knee. "Yall get this mess cleaned up while I make a few phone calls. It ain't gone take me long, and we'll get out to the old middle school. I wanna get there before Meyer does."

"I need to see a doctor," Kendall said, rolling off the couch and dropping to his knees.

"You can do that on yer own damn time."

"I need shots." Kendall reached his arm out and slung blood around the room. "Your dog might have rabies."

"Bullshit," Peanut said. "Marshall, shoot him full of Mud so he'll shut the fuck up."

"You got it," Marshall said, leaving the room, and Peanut started dialing a new number.

10.

I left the living room after Marshall came back with a syringe full of Country Mud, took a seat in one of the rocking chairs, and watched Andy come up the front porch steps and sit in the chair next to me. Kendall's voice carried through the screen door, he hollered for my brother not to stick him with the needle and fill him full of the drug, but his words got muffled. I imagined Caudell trapped Kendall's pleas inside his throat by clasping a hand over the man's mouth. Soon enough, the commotion inside turned still except for Marshall bitching about having to clean up more blood.

A tangerine glow spread across the northern sky, setting Blue Ridge Mountain peaks afire and chased the sun toward the west. Andy glared at me, her eyes a pair of cinder blocks stacked atop my chest, weighing me down, and trapping me in my seat. I distracted myself by cloud-gazing, keeping my eyes focused on the different shapes of condensation I picked out, and never let my stare lock on Andy's. She sat there until Peanut came around the corner of the house, Otis following close behind, soaking wet from a bath, and vanished when Peanut sat down.

Otis shook himself out on the porch, spraying us with

dog-scented water, and we threw our hands up to keep our faces from getting wet. Peanut sat the telephone on the arm of the rocking chair and said, "Dammit, Otis, cut that shit out and go lay down." He pointed at the far end of the porch where a mat was spread out for the dog, but Otis looked at Peanut as though the command didn't register and spun until he wound his body tight and laid at his master's feet. Peanut shook his head. "This damn dog don't listen."

"Kendall might not agree with that."

"Shit," Peanut grinned through a dip. "He ain't never gone look at a dog the same way again."

"Katie know you got him trained to do all that?"

"Mack, you know all my best ideas come from Katie."

"She's a terrifying woman."

"All the best ones are."

The creaking of the rocking chairs filled in the blank spaces our words left open, and Otis whacked his tail against the floor. His ears perked up, watching squirrels run across the yard but didn't twitch a muscle after Peanut said for him to stay.

I planted my feet, stopped rocking my chair, looked over at Peanut for the first time, saw his eyes were somewhere else, and brought him back to the present when I asked, "Why'd you lie to me?"

"I ain't lied to you."

"You did about knowing where the church is at."

"You ain't never asked me where the church is at."

"Don't get coy with me."

Peanut spat, wiped a lip with a knuckle, said, "I ain't being coy, Coy. Yer brother asked me where the church is, and I lied to him."

"Same difference," I said, digging my nails into the arm of the chair. "Lying to him is lying to me."

"You know why I lied about it, don't ya?"

I didn't answer the question.

"All right, I'll tell you why. Remember when I told you I wasn't gone have no part in helping you get Andy back? You went off guns blazing at that church and left a mess for me to clean up, did you not? Well, I knew if I told you I knew where yer mama's at, you wouldn't follow along with the plan I got. You'd've hauled ass over to TCC and bit off more than yer ass could chew. Would've got you and yer mama dead."

"I wouldn't've gone by myself."

"All right, you'd've got you and yer brother killed. Imagine me having to explain how stupid you are to yer deddy."

The screen door slapped open, and Caudell came out, hauling Kendall on a shoulder. A towel had got duct-taped over the arm Otis used for a chew toy, and his eyes were moonlit and unreachable, staring off into some faraway plane where sober eyes can't see. Drool dribbled from the corner of his mouth, and his head hung the way a balloon does after it starts deflating.

"Yall ready?" Peanut asked.

"Hell yeah, we are," Marshall said, coming out of the door after Caudell. "And don't yall worry about that blood. We got it cleaned up while yall sat out here and talked about yer feelings."

Peanut ignored my brother, hustling down the front porch steps to get to the Bronco before Caudell reached it. He unlocked the back hatch, lifting it for Kendall's body to get rolled inside. Marshall walked with me, and Otis followed along, keeping an eye peeled out for squirrels Peanut wouldn't let him chase.

"You nervous at all?"

"Do what?"

"About Mama."

"I don't guess so."

"I hope they ain't hurt her."

I shook my head. "Say your prayers for the man who even thinks of laying a finger on her."

"Just think if Deddy finds out."

"You ain't told him about this none at all?"

"Hell naw, you'd know he'd break outta Sweetwater and be here right now."

"Those Ghostface Devils wouldn't know what was coming."

"Sure as hell wouldn't."Marshall split off from me, went to the truck's driver's side, opened the door, and let Otis hop inside first. I got in next to the dog, and before Peanut cranked the Bronco, he spoke to us all in the rear-view mirror.

"All right, yall listen here. I put out a call to some buddies of mine who're going to meet us at the middle school. You ain't gone get to meet 'em or will even know they're there except for me telling yall they are. There won't be no need to go and get in a fight with the Devils because these boys will have our backs."

"How they gone do that?" I asked.

"Now, if I told you all the details, it'd ruin the surprise, wouldn't it?" Peanut smiled, reaching for his notebook of CDs on the dashboard, and flipped through it until he found the disk he wanted. He fed it to the stereo, and Waylon Jennings started singing about some good ol' boys.

The old middle school is where the four of us attended

junior high. Not long after we all graduated to high school, Tugalo County got the money to build a new one in town. For a time, the old middle school became an alternative center for the bad and special needs kids. But once it got shut down, it never got used again, and the building sat there abandoned, except when kids broke in, vandalizing the unoccupied classrooms, partying in the vacant lounges, or racing dirt bikes up and down the empty hallways. The school board did what they could to keep kids out but underestimated their enthusiasm for hellraising.

Peanut steered through the parking lot, eyeing kids along the way who recognized the baby blue SUV and cranked their pickups, and left when his gaze fell upon them. He circled the gymnasium and parked in the middle of the lot with the headlights facing the building. Peanut got out a cellphone, dialed a number, and the voice who answered said his men were ready. Peanut hung up the phone and turned up a song where Waylon sang about always being crazy.

We sat there listening to old country music, none of us saying a word, until Marshall sat up in his seat, leaned over Caudell's shoulder, and pointed out a white utility van coming around the building. Dents and scratches decorated the hood and sides of the van, a headlight was busted, and a crack in the windshield spiderwebbed from one side to the other. The van cruised until it got within throwing distance of the Bronco, circled behind us, and parked crossways, the sliding door on the passenger side facing us.

Peanut got out first, and the rest of us followed him, gathering together at the back end of the Bronco. Otis hopped over his seat, stood on Kendall's chest, and barked. We waited for movement from the utility van, and after none came, it got me wondering if we didn't drive into a trap. My eyes crisscrossed the tree line above us, looking for any sign of gunmen—a glint from a sight, colors that didn't blend in with the surroundings, or branches or leaves shaking and trembling from someone hiding.

My eyes snapped back to the van when the driver's side door opened, and Meyer got out. He came hoodless this time—dressed in a pair of black Dickies and work boots and wore a dingy wife beater to show off the tattoos decorating his arms and chest and neck. He walked slow, strutting around the front of the van with a smile playing at the corners of his mouth. His left eye was wine-colored, and claw marks ran from his socket and down his cheek.

Meyer noticed me studying the injury, pointed at it, and said, "You see this, boy? Yer mama's a fucking firecracker. What I ought to have done to her, I'm gonna take out on you."

Meyer stopped short when Peanut threw out an arm, stopped Marshall from charging across the parking lot, and opening a fresh can of whoop-ass on Mama's captor. Meyer's smile didn't play any longer. It spread across his face and came with laughter. He approached the sliding door and reached for the handle to fling it open when Peanut punched a fist in the air and called for him to stop.

Green lasers polka-dotted Meyer's chest and stomach, and he didn't have to get told to look down at them. He froze and got stiff all over the way a dead body does after rigor mortis sets in. His eyes were all that moved, the injured one twitching more than anything else, watching to see if Peanut would order him to get executed by firing squad.

Peanut separated himself from our group, approaching

Meyer the way he would a pile of dog shit, and said, "Let me go ahead and stop you 'fore you get ahead of yerself."

"I got their bitch mama in here like you asked."

"You call that woman a bitch again, and I'm gone have a hole blown in your chest so large I'll be able to go swimming in it."

Meyer sneered, said, "That'll have to be a large hole for a fat man like you."

"Ask your mama the kind of tight holes a fat man like me can fit in."

"My mama never gave two shits for me."

"Well, she'd have done us all a favor if she'd have turned out some crotchfruit salad instead of a walking, talking abortion."

Life returned to Meyer's limbs. He whacked the van's side panel with the palm of his hand and spoke between clenched teeth, "You wanna make this fucking trade or stand here and measure dicks?"

"Don't play games with me that you know you can't win."

Meyer's clenched teeth ground together, the muscles in his jaw got tense, and the veins in his neck bulged beneath tatted skin. His face turned red from the increased blood flow, and he stared death upon Peanut.

Peanut took another step forward, his fist still raised over his head, and said, "Be careful what you do next, son. If my arm drops to my side, you'll be dead before yer boys in that van can get a gun aimed in the right direction."

"What makes you think I got Devils in here ready to gun you down?" Meyer asked, his jaw muscles loosened so he could smile.

"You don't sit on the throne as long as I have without doing some thinking."

"You can't sit on that throne forever."

"I'll sit on it 'til I don't want to no more. Now, before you open that door, tell whoever's inside there not to let their balls get too big for their britches, or they'll end up squatting when they pee."

"Yall hear that?" Meyer asked. "Play nice when I open this door. We don't want Mr. Bohannon getting his feelings hurt."

Peanut waited until Meyer started getting antsy. He switched his weight from one foot to the other, the tension gone from his jaw muscles, his mouth hanging loose now, death no longer filling his eyes but instead percolated with worry. After I started wondering what Peanut's game was, he stepped back until he stood with the rest of us and said, "Open that door real slow. You do it too fast, and I'll drop my fist."

"I came here to make a switch with you."

"I know that."

"Then let me see if you got Kendall with you."

"I got Kendall with me."

"Let me see—"

"No," Peanut said, his voice hitting Meyer hard, knocking the words from his mouth. "We're playing by my rules. You give me Rhonda Dooley, and then I'll let you have Kendall. It ain't working no other way than that."

Meyer turned his back on us and opened the door, sliding it slow until it locked in place. Mama lay on the floor of the van. A group of men kneeled around her, guns pointed at the roof, their eyes watching Meyer for what to do next. He reached for Mama—a burlap sack covered her head, her were hands tied together and guided her out of the van. When her feet met the pavement, Meyer shoved her toward us, and she stumbled, skinning her knees.

Mama hopped to her feet before I could break away

from the group. She spun in circles, swinging her fists about, trying to knock the hell out of anybody who came close to her. I ducked low, snatched her up by the waist, and she flung her body about, fighting to get loose. Marshall came up next to us, yanked the sack away, and Mama relaxed when she saw who held her.

Peanut opened the Bronco's hatch when we got Mama to safety. Caudell drug Kendall out, dropped his body to the pavement, and left him lying there. Otis stood in the back of the truck, growling at the men across the parking lot from us, and barked when Meyer stepped forward. Meyer stopped short and raised his hands to his chest.

Peanut laughed, said, "You ain't scared of no dog, are you?"

"Is he dead?"

"Naw." Peanut looked down at Kendall. "Just medicated."

"You gonna let me have him?"

"You can get him once we leave. But, listen here, yer days of hanging around Tugalo County are over. Yall take this piece of shit and get the fuck outta my town. I hear word one of yall sneaking around, and next time these triggers get pulled. Understand?"

PART FOUR

HOMEGOING

1.

Weeks passed, an autumn chill moved in to replace the summer heat, and leaves changed from green to the color of a Southern sunset, and football season got into full swing. Caudell disappeared again, going to wherever Peanut asked him to, but Marshall stayed home, moved in with Mama, and kept an eye on her while she got over the shock of getting abducted. Marshall spent his days at Peanut's compound, drinking and planning ways to expand the empire, while my time got spent at the high school, scheming up game plans for the defense with an eye on Blackwood. Monty circled them on our calendar, and we wouldn't lose to them this year.

Jessa didn't complain about the amount of time I spent with the team. It made her happy to know I quit drinking and that our relationship was in the best place it'd been in the year and a half we'd been dating. We didn't go on dates every night, but we found some ways to make our time special: we cooked together and substituted grape juice for wine, sat out by a fire and tangled our bodies together in wool blankets, and watched Burt Reynolds movies we found on cable TV.

Despite my delicate grip upon sobriety, my visions of Andy did not go with the drinking. If anything, they intensified and became more frequent. She came to me at all hours, dressed in her Sunday best, expressing her unhappiness with me more often now than when she lived. Randy Jessup no longer accompanied her and only sometimes haunted my dreams. Andy became an entity separate from him and possessed my discernment of what was real and what was imagined. I learned to coexist between these worlds and functioned well enough that no one questioned my sanity. At least not those closest to me.

"Where's your head at, Coach?"

"Do what?"

I looked away from a computer monitor, footage of Blackwood's offense playing on loop, and saw Monty standing in the office doorway. He chewed bubble gum the way a major league pitcher does when the bases are fully loaded, and the batter who steps up to the plate can knock a ball into the stands. Monty dealt with his pregame jitters by smacking on a stick of Juicy Fruit. He'd spit it in the trash once we stepped into the tunnel and got ready to run onto the field. The boys waited for us in the locker room now, jeering one another and blasting OutKast so loud it rattled the office windows. It was almost game time, and we needed to give our pregame speeches.

"You're staring at that computer screen, but you ain't seeing what's on it."

I didn't answer, not wanting to say I saw Andy's face on Jessa's when I kissed her before she left to sit with her girlfriends.

Monty came over, sat on the corner of my desk, readjusted his ballcap, sitting it on the crown of his head, crossed his arms, and chomped his gum, his teeth clonking together. "Get your head in the game, Mack. This's Blackwood we're playing."

"You ain't gotta worry 'bout me, Coach. The defense is gone be ready."

"You're damn right they are. Them boys know this's the biggest game of the year." He jabbed his finger into the desktop for emphasis and leaned closer to me. "But I am worried about you, brother. Your mind's been somewhere else since you kicked the booze."

"Monty—"

"Hey, listen here, I just want you to know if you're struggling with thoughts of going back to the bottle, I'm here to help, understand?"

I closed out the footage of Blackwood's offense and flipped off the monitor. "We need to get to the locker room."

"Don't forget what I said." Monty clapped me on the shoulder, slid off my desk, led the way to the locker room, and one of the assistants turned off the music when Monty stepped inside, yelling for the team to hush and listen up.

Boys sat on the edge of pinewood benches fidgeting, clasping and unclasping their hands, eyes on the floor or the ceiling or staring straight at Monty, their legs bouncing with the adrenaline high already surging through their veins.

"I ain't gotta tell yall how big this game is. Yall go out there tonight, do your jobs, and get a W. This town can brag about it the whole rest of the year while Blackwood goes home embarrassed. Won't nothing make nobody happier than embarrassing Blackwood. Yall hear me? Go out there tonight, smash 'em in the mouth, and make sure they know they played some goddamn Titans!"

With his last words, the locker room erupted, and Monty walked out, leaving me to get the boys settled again. I rode the tide of their excitement—their shouts and chants punched my eardrums and rang in my gut, expelling dark thoughts from my mind and closing the void Andy occupied. When their eyes focused on me, and it got quiet enough to hear everybody breathing, I said, "Yall heard Coach, so what the fuck are we waiting on? Go out there and knock the hell outta the man in front of ya!"

Jessa scooted across my truck's bench seat, squeezed right up next to me, leaned her head onto my shoulder, and turned down the sports radio talking about Tugalo County's blowout win over Blackwood. She ran a hand between my thighs, squeezed the inside of my leg, and turned her head in to kiss my shoulder. I rested my head on top of hers and filled my lungs with the smell of her hair. We watched the road ahead of us, the truck's low beams shining just bright enough for us to see the double yellow line splitting the blacktop in two.

"Are you happy?"

Trees rushed by my open window, and the wind gusted outside, causing chill bumps to speckle my arms and neck.

"Do what?"

"You been quiet ever since we left. Thought you'd be more excited after getting a big win like that."

"I'm excited."

Jessa snuggled closer, hogging what little room got left between us. "How long's it been since Tugalo County beat Blackwood?"

"First win in five years."

"Yall got lucky."

"Say what now, girl?"

"I didn't wanna tell you this, but I paid off Coach Ransom to let yall get that win."

"You did, did ya?"

"Sure did."

"And why would you do that?"

"Because I love you."

I laughed, said, "Sometimes I question your Southerness."

Jessa pinched the inside of my thigh, and I jumped up in my seat, and she said, "Why would you even say that?"

"Because you know as well as I do, there ain't a Southerner alive who loves their significant other more than their football team."

My cell phone buzzed in the cupholder, interrupting our flirting the way an intrusive parent barges in on teenage sweethearts trying to take their romance a little too far.

Jessa reached down and grabbed it for me, but before she could tell me who called, I said, "Let that thing go to voicemail."

She flipped it open, checking the caller ID. "It's Peanut, sweetness."

"Why the hell is he calling?"

"Maybe you should answer it."

"I don't wanna talk to him."

"Mack." Jessa shoved the phone at me.

"All right, damn. Hand it here."

I took the phone from Jessa, mashed a green button, and put the phone to my ear. "Hello."

"Mack, don't argue with me about this, but you need to get yer ass over to the compound right now."

I dropped the phone in my lap and slammed both feet on the brakes.

2.

A white utility van with no driver behind the wheel blocked the road. Its side was dented and scratched like the one Meyer drove to the gymnasium, and now that I could see it closer, I noticed how the wheel wells had got eaten up with rust, and the bumper was missing from the back of the van. I could hear its engine humming over a serenade of bullfrogs, flipped on my high beams, and glanced all around for someone who might be hiding.

"What's going on here, Mack?"

I shifted into reverse without answering Jessa's question, stomped on the accelerator, and saw the van's sliding door fling open. A trio of men kneeled inside with automatic rifles aimed at my windshield. I put a hand across the back of Jessa's neck, shoved her toward the floor, and spun the steering wheel counterclockwise. A burst of gunfire lit the van's interior—bullets ricocheted off the blacktop and punched out my headlights. They clanged around the inside of the truck's engine, and cotton-white smoke blew from under the hood.

My truck's rear tires rolled through a ditch, and the back end went airborne, ejecting me from my seat, so my head knocked against the metal roof. When the law of gravity took hold, pulling the rear of my truck back toward the earth, the front end got aimed toward the heavens, and I got a passing view of the Milky Way before the front end came down hard, and I bit through my tongue, filling the inside of my mouth with the taste of rusty metal. Jessa tumbled into the floorboard, preventing her from smashing into the dash when my truck bed collided with a sycamore tree.

The force of impact launched me forward, ramming my chest into the steering wheel, and knocked the breath from my lungs. My vision went blank and white spots dotted my sight when it began to return. I saw the gunmen hopping their way down the hillside, and before I could reach for her, Jessa kicked her door open, slid out of the truck, and yanked my Remington 700 from behind the seat. She hunched low, braced her hip against the doorframe, and fired. The gunman to my right took a belly shot, dropped in a pile of leaves, clutching his gut, and did his best to keep his blood from spilling out. His buddies scattered, and Jessa disappeared around the truck.

Enough of my brains returned for me to throw the driver's side door open and snatch my tire knocker from under my seat. I rolled out, looking all around for someone to hit, but dropped to my stomach when I heard gunfire. I got back up when nobody hollered, kept low against the truck, and searched all around for Jessa but didn't see her. The girl posed a greater threat than me, and despite my worries for her safety, I resisted the urge to call out her name. It would do neither of us any good for me to get myself shot.

I snuck around the back end of the truck, did my best not to make any sound, and dropped to a knee when I heard leaves crunching. I got down low enough to glance beneath the undercarriage and saw a pair of worn-out boots shuffling my way. Once the gunman reached the taillights, I launched myself from a squat, brought the hitch-end of the thumper up like a spear, and rammed it underneath his chin. The gunman stumbled backward, squeezed the trigger out of reflex, spraying gunfire at the stars, and once he hit the ground, I was there before he regained his senses and smashed him in the face. His teeth shattered the way glass does when a rock gets thrown through it, and his nose crunched like a plastic bottle when it gets stepped on. The gunman's arms and legs went limp, but I bashed his face a second time, guaranteeing he wouldn't get up again.

My body froze when a voice sounding like sandpaper scraping over a raw piece of wood spoke out of the darkness and said, "Drop the nigger knocker in the dirt, boy."

Despite my brain telling me to do what the man said, I couldn't get my fingers to slacken. My grip tightened around the wooden handle of the thumper, and the muscles in my arms and shoulders strained as though I lifted something heavy. The man scuffled forward, kicking up leaves on his way over, jabbed a pistol barrel behind my ear, and said, "Don't make me repeat myself."

"You best aim that gun somewhere else."

The man looped an arm around my ribcage, squeezed me against his chest, spun us in the direction of Jessa's voice, and said, "Hey, girl! Why don't you come on out so I can see ya. I've heard yer real pretty."

"I'd rather roll in dog shit than let you look at me."

"Don't be a bad sport now." The man laughed. "Not when I got a gun aimed at this boy's head."

Jessa stepped out from behind a beech tree, the

moonlight illuminating her figure and appearing like a guardian angel.

"Well," the man said. "They wasn't lying. I would be a whole lot more comfortable if you dropped that gun."

"Not until it blows your brains out."

The man's arms flexed, and he raised his voice. "Listen, girl, that mouth's only got one use, and it ain't for talking."

This time Jessa laughed. "Sorry, hon, ain't no way I'd ever give head to a man who's got War Damn Eagle tattooed on his neck."

"You dumb bitch—"

I swung the hitch-end of the thumper over my shoulder, breaking the rusty steel off in the man's mouth, so he swallowed his words and dropped his gun. He sat down hard on his ass, covered his mouth with both hands, and screamed into them. I raised the knocker in the air to bash the gunman's brains out, but before I could follow through on the downswing, his chest exploded from a bullethole, knocking him flat on his back.

Jessa came up next to me, the Remington aimed at the dying gunman's forehead, and said to him, "I told you I'd blow your brains out."

"Let him suffer, Jessa," I said, reaching over and putting a hand on the rifle.

I could feel her tension through the cold steel of the barrel, and when I thought she'd pull the trigger, she handed the Remington over to me, leaned in close so I could put an arm around her, and sighed.

We stood that way until the gunman quit breathing and went looking for my cell phone.

3.

I found my cell phone under the bench seat in a pile of broken glass and saw I had missed calls from Peanut and my brother. Jessa sat on the truck's front bumper with her back to me, chewing on her fingernails. She wanted to get out of these woods, so I waited to return the calls. I came around to her, looped an arm through hers, and led her back to the road. We didn't speak on our way up the hill, and when we got to the van, she walked over to it without me telling her we should take it, got in through the open door, slid it shut behind her, and climbed into the passenger's seat.

I dialed Marshall's number on my way around to the driver's side and didn't have to wait long for him to answer. "You all right, Coy? I got a call from Peanut telling me to get Mama and me over to the compound because the Ghostface Devils are on the warpath."

"They just tried ambushing me and Jessa on the way home from the game."

"Goddammit, are yall all right?"

"I'm standing here talking to you, Marshall."

"How's Jessa?"

"She did most of the killing," I sighed. "She's pretty shook up from it."

"You need to go ahead and marry that girl. It's the only way you can pay her back for all the times she's saved your ass."

"I'm not really thinking about marriage right now," I said, opening the driver's side door and sliding the Remington in behind the seat. Jessa stared straight ahead and didn't flinch when I slammed the door. "You got Mama over to the compound?"

"Just got here. She's got supper cooking with Katie, and I'm standing here with Peanut."

"Katie's got supper cooking?"

"You know Katie ain't fixing to let a war stop her from hosting guests."

"How's Mama?"

"Fine. And if she's scared, she ain't showing it."

"All right, I'm gone letcha go. We're fixing to head that way."

"Be careful, Coy. See you when you get here," Marshall said and hung up.

Jessa turned to me after I flipped my phone shut. She reached across the van and stopped me from shifting it into drive. Her eyes gleamed in the starlight above us, and shadows formed around the angles of her face. She looked like a dream attempting to tear through the curtain of sleep and come to life. "You're thinking about marrying me?"

"I was hoping you didn't hear that."

"Answer the question."

"Jessa, after all the bullshit we just dealt with, it ain't at the forefront of my mind right now."

"But you been thinking 'bout it?"

"Here and there I have."

"Mack," Jessa said my name like cinder blocks were tied to it, "the two of us both agreed we wasn't interested in having nothing more than a one-night stand."

"Well, you do know that one-night stands usually only last for one night, right?"

"Don't nitpick my words. You know I ain't trying to get tied down by no man."

"Jessa, there ain't a man alive who wants to tie you down less than me."

4.

I steered onto the dirt road leading to Peanut's compound. He had gotten a new gate installed, and this time, he had security cameras mounted at either end of it and some new guards waiting to let us in. Neither man came over to the van to speak, but I recognized one of them from when I worked at my uncle's furniture shop. Buddy Slaughter did a nickel in Sweet Water for not stopping his bass boat when the law ordered him to and made them chase him around Lake Ayers twice. Buddy told the court he would've kept the chase going if the boat hadn't run out of gas.

I waved at Buddy after he winked at me and drove through the gate once it was open. Albermarle Mountain overshadowed the property like a broken heart overshadows fond memories of the past. Its blinking radio towers guided me to Peanut's house, and I parked next to my brother's truck. Marshall waited on the front porch and came down to meet us in the driveway. He brought a couple of cans of Coors with him, handing one of them to Jessa, and kept the other for himself, leaving me with nothing to drink.

"Katie's got some Co-Cola inside for you, Coy."

"Couldn't've brought a can out for me?"

"Shit, my hands was full," Marshall said, leading us back to the house.

Jessa hooked an arm through mine, took a swig of beer, and said hey to Peanut when he came outside. Mama followed him out, Katie came next, and Otis came after her. The dog barreled down the steps, almost falling over itself, and greeted me with a nose in my crotch. After he caught my scent, he moved onto Jessa and rolled onto his back, and she stooped down to rub his belly.

"Where the hell did you get that van?" Peanut asked, spitting a string of dip into a plastic bottle.

"Drove my truck into a tree trying not to get shot. Wrecked it all to hell."

"My God," Mama said, coming down the steps. She grabbed me by the face, dug her fingernails into my beard, and looked me all over. "You all right, son?"

"Just banged up."

Mama turned to Jessa. "You okay, girlie?"

Jessa smiled. "Yes, ma'am. Just banged up a little like Mack said."

"Where's ya truck at now, Mack?"

"Out on Walton Creek Road. Couple miles down from the trailer. It's sitting off in the woods."

"Leave any trash behind?"

"There's some that needs to get thrown away."

Peanut nodded. "I'll have a garbage man go take care of it. He'll take somebody with him to have a look at the truck. If he can get it running, I'll have it fixed up for ya. If not, I'll give ya something new."

"You ain't gotta do that," I said, waving off Peanut's words.

"You got something parked in the garage at home?"

I didn't answer.

"That's what I thought."

"Yall hungry any at all?" Katie asked. "Your Mama made up her chicken and dumplings, and I got cornbread and fried okra to go with it."

"Hell, Katie's been making me wait for yall to get here 'fore she'll let me eat," Peanut said, scooping his dip out of his mouth and flinging it out into the yard.

"Patience is something good for you to learn, Sweet Pea. Don't know how many years of our marriage I've been trying to teach it to you."

Katie led us all into the house, sent Peanut to the dining room to get the table set and let me and Jessa fix our bowls first. My appetite went into a frenzy when I got a whiff of Mama's chicken and dumplings. I filled my bowl to the rim and piled the cornbread on top of it. Peanut came into the kitchen, saw my bowl, and said, "Damn, Mack, save some for the rest of us."

Katie knuckled Peanut's bicep, said, "He can have as much as he wants."

I took a seat at a walnut-colored table, and Jessa sat down next to me. She spread a napkin over her lap, sat up tall with her back straight, and placed her hands on her knees, waiting for everybody else. When I went ahead and started eating, Jessa snuck a hand across the space separating us, and pinched the back of my arm. I couldn't yell for choking on my food and rubbed the skin where it hurt. She cut her eyes over at me, telling me to have some damn manners without saying it aloud.

Marshall came into the dining room next, bringing me a Coke, and everyone filed in after him. Once they all got seated, Katie looked across the table at us and said, "Yall didn't have to wait on us. Go ahead and eat."

I cut my eyes over at Jessa this time, but she ignored me.

After we all emptied our bowls, Mama got up and started clearing the table. Katie argued with her, saying a guest shouldn't have to clean, but Mama didn't listen.

Peanut reached over, put a hand on Katie's arm, said, "Will you make Deddy up a bowl and take it out to him? I'm sure he ain't ate all day."

"I'm already making it," Mama said. "Heading out the back door now."

"Good God," Peanut said. "The woman ain't stopped from the second she got here."

"She's working off some of that anxiety," Marshall said. "That's why she's going out to see Deddy."

"Good Lord, Peanut," Katie said. "Keep that kinda mess to yourself."

"Do what now?" Jessa asked, shock in her voice.

Marshall propped his elbows on the table, leaned into it, staring over at me, and said, "You ain't told Jessa that Mama's been sneaking around with Buford?"

I shook my head.

"Been worse than a couple of teenagers figuring out what fits where."

"Peanut, I'm fixing to smack the hell outta you," Katie said. "I better not hear you talking like that around the boys."

"Why ain't you told me?" Jessa asked me.

"Hell, I've been in damn denial over it."

"Does your Deddy know?"

"Oh, hell no," Marshall spoke over me. "He ain't gone know either. His ass would break outta Sweet Water right now if he did. He'd kill everybody at this table for not telling him."

"Well," Jessa said, "good for your Mama, I guess."

Peanut shoved away from the table, grabbed the back

of Katie's chair, and stood. "Yall boys wanna go outside with me and have a dip?"

5.

When Peanut led us outside, a whole crew of men kept a watch over the house. Two men were posted at the front porch steps, two more stood at either end of the porch, and another two were out in the yard, making rounds around the house. I didn't recognize any of their faces, letting me know that Peanut didn't trust any locals and went outside Tugalo County for help. The men were all dressed in black with tactical vests on, guns and knives holstered on their hips, and rifles slung over their shoulders. They never acknowledged our presence and went about their business like we didn't exist.

Peanut took a seat in his favorite rocking chair and waited for me and Marshall to join him. An October chill was in the air, but it wasn't biting, and I could sit outside without wearing heavy clothes. I took a seat on Peanut's right, waved off the can of dip when he offered it and got out one of my own. He raised his eyebrows at me, not saying he was surprised at my new habit. We packed our cans and shoved large pinches inside our bottom lips. Marshall sat down, sipping on a can of beer, keeping an eye on the men watching over us.

"It looks like you're getting ready to start a war, Peanut," I said.

"The fuck I am. I'm getting ready to end it." He spat in Katie's azaleas and rocked his chair hard so the wood whined under his weight.

"Don't look like the Ghostface Devils have kept their end of the bargain."

"Mack, I know you like making smartass comments when you're stressed out, but I ain't in no damn mood for it."

"And you get ill-natured when you're stressed out."

"Yall sound like a bickering-ass couple," Marshall said.

"What happened out in them woods, Mack?" Peanut asked, sitting forward, a violent gleam in his eyes.

I told the story, starting with the van blocking the roadway and ending with Jessa blowing a hole in the last gunman's chest.

Peanut chuckled, a grin curled the corners of his mouth, and the violent gleam in his eyes lost some of its sparkle. "How many times has that girl done saved your ass now? You been keeping count, right, Marshall? Tell your brother he needs to go ahead and marry her 'fore she takes that good luck elsewhere."

Marshall sat up, a serious look on his face, said, "Hold up, now, you said you broke Deddy's thumper?"

"Broke the hitch off in a Devils' mouth."

"Damn, Coy, that thing's been in the family forever."

"It ain't a damn heirloom you pass down to your kids, Marshall."

"I'm just saying. It does got a little sentimental value to it."

"Yall calm down," Peanut said. "I'll see if I can have it fixed."

It got quiet on the front porch except for the rocking chairs. Marshall went back to watching Peanut's guards, and Peanut got a gravedigger's look on his face.

"What's with all the firepower, Peanut?" I broke the silence.

"Well," he sighed. "The shit, as they say, has done hit the fan."

"What do you mean?"

"Kendall Murdoch is dead."

"Do what?"

"The hell you say?" Marshall said.

"I found out right before I called the two of yall. Word got to me through a boy I got in the GBI. Said the Ghostface Devils drug Kendall outta his house naked, nailed his ass to a tree with some railroad spikes, and set him on fire."

"Just like they did Butcher Blake's nephew," Marshall said.

"Shit, worse than that. Doused him in lighter fluid from head to toe and lit him up like they were fixing to roast some fucking marshmallows," Peanut said. "Told me Kendall's screams got all his neighbors outside, and when that Meyer bastard saw he had an audience, he shot Kendall twice in the face. Left him in that tree burning until his wife came running outside with a fire extinguisher. Kendall's neighbors didn't do nothing but stand around and watch him smolder. They got Amelia in a hospital right now for fear she'll kill herself."

"Goddamn," Marshall said.

"Goddamn is right," Peanut agreed.

I pointed at the men surrounding us. "How'd you get them here so fast?"

"Speed dial."

"Don't bullshit me, Peanut."

"I ain't bullshitting no-fucking-body."

"You expected this to happen?"

"Hell no, I didn't expect it to happen. Do you know what them sumbitches done did? They ain't just got an enemy in me now. They've got an enemy in the whole state of Georgia. The whole fucking country. You can't go around setting a goddamn politician on fire without all of Uncle Sam's weight coming down on ya. It's the first lesson our deddys taught us."

I sat back in my rocking chair. This news made my dip taste like I'd packed my lip full of sawdust. I dug my finger through my bottom lip and flung the tobacco out into the yard. "What the hell's next?"

Peanut didn't answer. He got up out of his chair and said for us to follow him.

6.

We followed Peanut around the house, and one of the guards came with us. He led us to a sheet metal work building, unhooked a ring of keys from a belt loop, unlocked a steel door, let me and Marshall inside, and told the guard to wait for us. Fluorescent lights blazed on, burning white spots on my eyes, and I saw Andy sitting on a table workbench, smiling at me.

She wore a lavender dress with a lilac print and had her hair fixed up in a messy bun. Her feet dangled a foot above the floor, and she had her toes painted so they matched her dress. Andy's eyes locked on mine, robbing my brain of time and place. My surroundings faded the same way memories do after they get shoved to the back of someone's mind, never to get thought of again, leaving Andy and me alone, existing in that place where spirits must wait before they cross over from life to death or vice versa.

Andy stood before me now, her eyes still locked on mine, perusing my thoughts the way a mother does when sneaking a read of her daughter's diary. She reached a hand up, placing it on my cheek, though I sensed her touch more than felt it, and her good-natured expression turned mournful. Whatever we could have shared in life was unavailable to us now, and it hurt her to know I sought the love of someone else. I opened my mouth to explain how she could never lose her home in my heart and that Jessa would become a fellow occupant, but the words wouldn't form. My brain got snatched back into place, and I found myself standing in the middle of Peanut's work building, my brother next to me, asking where the hell I'd gone.

Peanut stepped up next to me, asked, "You tripping on me right now, Mack?"

"I ain't tripping."

"Damn sure seems that way."

"You know I ain't never done that shit."

"There was that one time in high school," Marshall said. "You spent the whole weekend in a tree thinking you were Batman or some shit. I don't exactly remember. Me and Brystal got so high we were walking on Saturn's rings."

"Goddamn." Peanut smirked. "Yall must not have invited me to that party."

"You had your head up Hannah Morrison's cooch at the time. Didn't want to hang out with us no more."

"Shit, Hannah Morrison would still have a warm spot in my bed if Katie hadn't never come along."

"Whatever happened to ol' Hannah?"

"Doesn't matter. I didn't bring yall out here to stroll down memory-fucking-lane."

Peanut waved us over to the workbench. I approached it with caution, afraid of getting close to the spot where Andy had sat moments before and getting transported back to that astral plane and having to see her mournful expression again.

Peanut turned to see what took me so long and said, "It's all right, Mack. Ain't nobody in no hurry here. I plan to be out here all damn night."

For the first time, I noticed 20-pound bags of fertilizer stacked on top of the table. Marshall lifted one, read its label, asked, "You getting ready to do some gardening or some shit?"

I came up beside my brother, took the bag from him, and held it like it would give me some insight into Peanut's plan.

"You know I ain't fixing to do no damn gardening," Peanut said. He hefted a bag onto a shoulder, told us to follow him, and led us to the back of his work building, where he dropped the bag at a bay door. Me and Marshall both dropped our bags on top of his and unlocked the far end of the door. Peanut lifted it open where a pickup had been parked with a pair of 55-gallon drums bungee cabled together in the bed.

The scene got me even more confused. "What the hell you planning, Peanut?"

"Mack, you remember our sixth-grade language arts teacher?"

I shook my head. "I don't know if I do or not."

"Yeah, the hell you do. You had a crush on the woman at the time and told her you wanted to grow up and be the next Stephen King. She thought that was the cutest fucking thing."

"You talking 'bout Miss Hinton?"

"That's her."

"I don't remember telling her I wanted to be the next Stephen King."

"Shit, I remember that. You told her you hated reading, so she gave you a buncha his books, and you came back and told her you wanted to grow up and be a writer like him."

"You did go through a Stephen King phase," Marshall said.

"Yeah, I remember reading all his books. What's that got to do with anything?"

"The books ain't got nothing do with nothing," Peanut said. "But you remember where Miss Hinton was from?"

"Wasn't it somewhere out in the Midwest?"

"Sure as hell was. Oklahoma City to be exact."

A smile a country mile long spread across Peanut's face, and a viciousness lit up his eyes, turning my spine into an icicle, setting me to shivering.

"Yall remember what happened in OKC?"

Marshall looked at me, expecting me to answer. When I didn't, he said, "I don't."

"You wouldn't," Peanut said. "You were too young. Me and yer brother there were in class on the day that I'm talking 'bout. Miss Hinton had us all reading *A Wrinkle in Time* when ol' Mr. Harris come barging in the room. Asked her if she had the TV on at all, and she said he was interrupting our reading assignment. He said she needed to have a look at the news because all anybody was talking about was OKC. It got quiet as a pin drop in that fucking room. You could feel all over your skin that something was wrong. It gives me chills right now to talk about it."

Peanut held his arm out for us to see the hair standing on ends and the goose pimples dotting his skin. "Miss Hinton got to shaking and couldn't get the remote to work. Mr. Harris had to come and take it from her, and when he flipped on the news, there was nothing but smoke and fire and a building that wasn't nothing but a big ass hole in the ground. Looked like a damn meteor had fallen outta the sky and just clobbered the sumbtich. Miss Hinton fainted right on the fucking spot. Had to get the school nurse up to her classroom to make sure she was all right. She didn't come back to school for a fucking week."

"What the hell are you getting at, Peanut?"

"Boys," Peanut slapped the back end of the truck, said, "We're fixing to Timothy McVeigh the Ghostface Devils."

7.

C oy! Hey, Coy!" Marshall hollered. "Wait up now, dammit."

After we finished filling Peanut's steel drums with the ammonium nitrate, I left the sheet metal building for the house. I'd done got tired, was ready to see Jessa, and wanted to get in bed. My nerves got my whole self to thrumming the way a guitar string does when it's wound too tight, and I yearned for a drink and needed to get away from the bomb Peanut built before I started sipping on the peach-flavored moonshine he was getting drunk on now.

Andy walked beside me; her lavender toes gleamed in the moonlight and gave me a look of consternation for not paying any attention to her. Her eyebrows drew together, her mouth made a hard line, and a vein pulsated on the left side of her neck from blood rushing to her face. She didn't break her stare until she heard Marshall's boots kicking up grass and didn't disappear as I expected her to when my brother caught up to us. He grabbed me by the arm, turned me in his direction, and couldn't speak for having to catch his breath.

I yanked my arm away from him and continued my

trek to the house, but my brother grabbed me by the shirt and wouldn't let go.

"Marshall," I shoved him off me, "I'm fixing to knock the shit outta you."

"Do it and see if these guards ain't gotta peel my ass off of ya."

"What kinda bug's done got up your ass?"

"You acting like you're hard of hearing."

"I don't feel like talking right now, goddammit."

"Well," Marshall stabbed a finger into the center of my chest, "you're gone have to after what you just agreed to."

"Did it sound like Peanut was giving me any other choice?"

"You didn't even try arguing with him."

"There wasn't no argument to get made."

"Bullshit." Marshall grabbed a handful of my shirt when I tried walking away. "When have you not argued with Peanut over the smallest fucking details of any plans he tries to make?"

"Maybe it's something I wanna do."

"The hell it is. I can tell by the look on your god-damn face."

"Just drop it, Marshall."

"You ain't gotta do this, Coy." My brother twisted my shirt around his fist until it pulled me close to him, and we stood nose to nose.

"I'm driving that truck tomorrow, and that's all there is to it."

"Do you got a death wish or something? I mean, what the hell?"

Andy stepped into my line of sight after Marshall fin-ished asking the question. Her eyes invited me to meet her back at the place she'd taken me to earlier in the night.

Questions of life or death didn't matter there, and we could exist apart from the stress and anxiety of what went on in this world, but my mind couldn't break away from reality because Marshall shook me as though I'd fallen into a coma.

I put my hands on my brother's shoulders, pushed him back a step or two, getting him far enough away so we didn't have to smell each other's breath, and said, "Marshall, we gotta get up early as hell in the morning. Let me get up to Jessa and see her 'fore she's done asleep, all right?"

Marshall unwound his fist from my shirt, not saying a word when he turned back to the sheet metal building and left me standing with Andy in the middle of the yard. She looked relieved to see him gone, and her eyes extended the invitation to join her in that astral world once more but disappeared when I didn't immediately agree to come.

Back inside the house, everything was quiet. A hallway light let me see enough to not trip over any toys on my way to the staircase, and when I made it to the second floor, I eased open the door to the room me and Jessa shared, doing my best not to make the hinges squeak.

Jessa sat up in the bed after I closed the door behind me. She laid under nothing but the sheet, it slid down to just above her breasts, and she placed a palm over it, holding it there. The girl looked like a scene from out of a movie, and I couldn't bring myself to move from where I stood for fear of my brain not having enough time to capture the image and store it away in my memories.

"I didn't know if you were ever gone come to bed."

"I been trying to get up here to see you for the last thirty minutes."

"Why you just standing there like that?"

"So I don't ever forget the way you look."

"Why don't you come here and let me give you some-thing else to remember."

I kicked off my shoes, undressed on the way to the bed, got under the sheet with my girlfriend, and never told her about the bomb I'd be driving the next morning.

8.

I flung myself out of bed naked when the bedroom door hurled open. A brick wall of a figure filled the doorway and swayed on his feet as if he stood on a pontoon, unable to get his footing right. He took a step back from me, held out a hand, signaling for me not to charge him, and grabbed ahold of the doorframe to keep himself steady.

When Peanut spoke, his words came out slurred, "Getcha some goddamn clothes on, Mack. Damn, I don't wanna see none of that." Peanut turned away from me, using the door to block his view of my pecker. "I hope you ain't up here doing what it looks like. Damn, that's my son's bed, man. Gone have to get Katie to wash them sheets now."

"What the hell you doing barging into this room like you're the goddamn law for?"

"Hey, now," Peanut came back into the room, keeping a throttlehold on the doorknob. "I own this goddamn house in case you done forgot. I'll barge into any fucking room I want."

I hopped around, trying to get my pants on, stumbled into the bed, and set Jessa to stirring.

"Damn, Mack, you done snuck a sip of my hooch? Can't hardly stand up, can ya?"

I shushed Peanut, not wanting to wake Jessa up, grabbed my cellphone, flipped it open, and checked the time. "We still got another two hours 'fore we gotta be anywhere with that truck."

"Yeah, I know," Peanut said, speaking so low I strained to hear him. "But the truck's gone."

"The hell you say?"

"Yer brother's done took the truck, Coy."

"Oh, fuck me. Why didn't you lead with that shit, Peanut?"

He waved a hand around, said, "I didn't expect to come in here and have to see your wang flopping around. Ain't never gone get that sight outta my brain now. Don't help none that I'm drunk neither."

I yanked my shirt over my head, shoved my feet into my boots, and guided Peanut into the hallway. "Well, c'mon. Let's go stop my brother 'fore he does something stupid."

"You know what he's gone do, right?" Peanut asked, leaning into a wall. "Gone take it to where them Devils are and blow their asses right up Satan's bunghole."

I stuck my head inside the bedroom, made sure Jessa hadn't woken up, pulled the door shut—afraid of the slightest sound disturbing her—and didn't breathe until the door latch clicked. "My whole family is gone end up in Sweetwater cause of your dumbass," I said, letting Peanut sling an arm over my shoulders.

"Ah hell, they ain't no way I'll let either one of yall go there. Yall are the closest thing I ever got to having brothers. Only reason yer deddy's there is cause he wants to be."

After we got downstairs, I steered Peanut over to the kitchen table and let him collapse into one of the chairs.

He sat down with a hard thud, groaned about how his head swam and sat over with his head between his knees.

"I hope to God you ain't fixing to throw up," I said.

"Naw, I just need a minute to get my head right."

"Where's your keys at? We can't go driving that utility van around."

"They're over there on the hook." Peanut pointed.

I grabbed his Bronco's keys from the hook next to the backdoor and said for him to come on.

"You ain't gone give me no hand?"

"Not this damn time. You're too heavy."

"Katie's been trying to get me to go on a diet."

"Maybe you oughta listen to her."

Otis got to barking when he heard the backdoor open, came running from the other side of the house and walked between us. The night had done got cold with October letting way to November, and I wished I wore something warmer than my Tugalo County coaching gear. Peanut's hired guns took notice of us leaving the house but made no moves to stop us. A man stationed on the far side of the porch spoke into a walkie-talkie clipped on his shoulder, and his men went back to patrolling the property.

Peanut beat me to the Bronco's driver's side and tried getting in behind the wheel, but I grabbed ahold of his arm, keeping him from hefting his weight into the seat. "Get your ass over to the other side of the truck. You damn sure ain't driving with as drunk as you are."

"I ain't too drunk to drive."

"You know who says that?"

"Who?"

"A drunk asshole."

Peanut's face darkened in the moonlight, his ballcap

shading his features. "I don't let nobody but Caudell drive this truck."

"Add me to the list then."

Peanut wobbled getting out of the Bronco, came toward me, and laughed, turning on his heel. "Should've seen the look on yer face," he said, going around the front of the truck. "Thought you was gone have to fight me, didn't ya?"

I ignored his taunting, used the steering wheel to pull myself into the seat, and Otis jumped in from the other side, sitting right next to me. The stereo blasted Dixieland Delight when I got the Bronco started. Peanut added some out-of-tune vocals to the song and cussed when I turned the music down. "The hell you did that for?"

"They can hear you all the way over in Chattooga right now."

Peanut rolled his window down instead of arguing, hung his head outside the truck, and let the cold air blast him in the face. He hollered for Buddy Slaughter to get the gate open when we rolled up to it, Buddy hustled at the sound of Peanut's voice, and I stopped the Bronco after pulling through.

Buddy came up to Peanut's side of the truck after locking the gate and leaned into the window to hear me speak. "How long ago was it when my brother came through here?"

"Not too long ago," Buddy said. "Ain't got no watch on me, but I reckon it was about 20- or 30-minutes past."

I drove off without saying thanks, and Peanut waved.

Peanut started giving me directions, said I needed to drive faster if we were going to catch up to Marshall, and that he wouldn't drive so slow if he were the one behind the wheel. I hammered my foot down on the accelerator, not worried about getting pulled over because any cop who saw Peanut sitting in the passenger's seat wouldn't even bother issuing us a warning.

After Peanut got us off the backroads, I asked, "What did you mean when you said Deddy's in Sweetwater cause he wants to be?"

Peanut sat in his seat, his window cracked, breathing steady and looking almost asleep. When he spoke, it was in a somber tone, as though he were a doctor getting ready to give a patient a life-altering diagnosis. "Mack, that really oughta be a conversation you have with Walter, but I'll tell you this much. He's there because he thought it'd be the best way to do by you and your brother. Yer mama wanted him to get out of this life and set a better example, and he thought the best example was not to be around at all."

"And Mama's curled up next to Buford right now."

"Hey, talk however you want about my damn deddy, but yer mama is too good a woman to get talked down on."

We didn't speak again until Peanut needed to give me more directions, his finger getting stuck over the dash and his words catching in his throat when we saw fire blazing over the treetops.

"Oh, fucking hell," Peanut said, shoving Otis back between us when the dog tried sticking his nose out of the window to catch a scent of the smoke.

"Goddammit."

"Don't turn around. Drive on up and see what we can find out."

"They got the whole sheriff's department here, Peanut. You really want them knowing we came nosing around?"

"Ain't nobody gone say shit to me."

I let the Bronco coast until we reached a barricade. A deputy stepped out into the middle of the road, holding up a hand, motioning for me to turn around. When I didn't do it, he shined a flashlight in my eyes and knocked a fist on the hood of the Bronco, demanding I leave the scene. Peanut told me to sit steady until the deputy came over to my window, and then he'd take it from there.

The deputy did like Peanut said he would, and before he could speak, Peanut leaned over Otis, filling the open space between us, speaking to the deputy the way he would a subordinate who wasn't worth his time. "Get Darryl Tracy out here and tell him to get some giddy-up in it. He's got some explaining to do."

The deputy got on his radio, yelling for Darryl Tracy's assistance, telling Darryl the situation on his hands was above his pay grade.

Darryl came hustling out of the trees, wearing a Tugalo County Sheriff's Department ball cap instead of a Stetson, a t-shirt instead of his regular button-up, looking like a man who'd just caught his daughter getting pretzeled by a high school boyfriend. His eyes caught a spark when he saw the Bronco and started flickering when he saw me behind the wheel. Peanut didn't give him a chance to speak. He said, "What you know good, Darryl?"

"I got the damn apocalypse on my hands, and you got me up here wasting time for what?"

Peanut looked out the windshield, watched the smoke rise over the trees, and said, "Me and Mack were up having a late-night beer, listening to the scanner, and heard about an explosion. We drove out here to see what the hell happened?"

"An explosion happened. Now I need to get back down there and sort through about a dozen dead men. Excuse me if I don't say have a good night."

"Hey, Darryl."

"What?"

"Any idea who they are?"

Darryl came all the way up to the driver's side door, rested his hands on it, and leaned inside the window. He got so close I had to sit back and spoke in a strangled voice, "I think you know exactly who they are."

9.

fter I got the Bronco turned around, Peanut said, "We need to go find yer goddamn brother."

"You got any idea where he might be?" I asked, mashing my foot on the accelerator, the Bronco's engine rumbling, building its way to its top speed.

Peanut shifted in his seat, his face a picture of sobriety now, pointing out the next turn he wanted me to take. "I got a couple of ideas, but that don't mean Marshall's gone be there. He's got to know what kinda stupid shit he just did. He'll be gone from Tugalo County if he's got his head thinking right."

"That's some stupid shit you were gone have me do."

"Naw, the hell I wasn't. It's a job I meant for Buddy Slaughter. I just wanted to fuck with you some 'fore in the morning."

I slapped the steering wheel, said, "You got to be fucking kidding me."

"You ain't gotta say shit, Mack." Peanut pounded a fist into the door, scaring Otis, the dog scooting close to me, almost into my lap. "I shouldn't've been drinking the fucking moonshine. Katie's been telling me I need to lay off of it."

"Then why don't you fucking listen to her."

I eased onto the brakes, slowing the Bronco down just

enough for me to steer onto the next road Peanut pointed out. We drove North, higher into the foothills of the Blue Ridge Mountains, and the world got a different feeling about it. The early morning chill turned cold, and moonglow was all we had to see by, lending a spookiness to our surroundings.

"Ain't no way Marshall could've made it this far on foot."

"I hope to God you don't think yer brother is that goddamn stupid." Otis whined at Peanut's tone and got shoved away when he tried licking Peanut in the face. "He would know better than to do some shit like that. You think he's hiding out in the woods right now like he's Eric fucking Rudolph?"

I didn't say nothing, but I could feel Peanut's glare on me, the weight of it made my foot heavy, and I drove those mountains roads faster, not slowing down any when I came to dog-eared turns.

"I can tell you right now, if you wreck my truck for driving like some maniac, you're gone have a helluva time getting my foot outta yer ass."

I turned to Peanut, but before I could get any words out, I saw his eyes brighten, he braced himself against his door, and I couldn't stop the Bronco from going sideways. The wheels skidded along the shoulder, kicking up dirt and gravel, tearing through grass, and finally veered into a groove I couldn't steer out of, cannonballing the truck downhill.

The Bronco's grill plowed through limbs and branches, a headlight busted, cracks spiderwebbed their way across the windshield, the truck bounced its way through ruts in the hillside, and my stranglehold on the steering wheel was all that kept me in my seat. I stomped both feet onto the brake pedal, but the Ford's momentum launched it forward, the front end of the Bronco smashed into an oak tree, and my face ate the steering wheel, cracking my vision and blacking it out.

Once my sight returned, I found myself laying atop damp earth, pine needles and grass stuck to my arms and shirt. My body moved the way a football player does after getting trucked once too often and couldn't have rolled over if not for a boot toe kicking me in the ribs. All my weight balanced on my elbows and knees, I dry heaved until long ropes of spit dangled from the corners of my mouth and fell on my side from a second blow.

I laid on my back, bracing myself against a boot heel stomping me into the dirt until I thought my chest would collapse and could finally breathe when my assailant planted his feet on either side of me. My attacker bent at the waist, getting close enough for me to see the upside-down cross tattooed across his forehead. His eye was still bloodshot from Mama almost clawing it out, and his breath smelled like he'd eaten a stink bug's asshole.

"What'd I tell you, boy? What'd I fucking tell you?"

"Call me boy again."

"What'd you say?" Meyer leaned closer, right in my face where I could grab him by the ears. "Speak up like a goddamn man."

I lunged forward, grabbed Meyer by the back of the head, laced my fingers together so that he couldn't pull away, and bit down on his fucking nose. He thrashed about, fighting to shove me off, but I tightened my grip, chomped down harder, and the taste of pennies filled my mouth. Meyer pummeled my body with hard fists, delivering heavy blows to my ribs and chest, clamped his fingers around my neck, and stabbed his thumbs into the soft spot below my Adam's apple.

I did my best not to unclench my teeth, but my inability to breathe made my jaws weaken, and I opened my mouth, gasping for air. Meyer jerked his head backward and slung it forward, smashing his forehead into my nose, cracking the bone, and my blood spewed like water from a busted pipe. My vision splintered, and I saw Andy standing all around me, looking down on me with her pretty eyes. She reached a hand out to me, tugged my heart toward the middle space she occupied now, and beckoned me to join her. I unlaced my fingers from around Meyer's head and clawed at the eye Mama had already damaged. He let out a deep howl, sounding like an injured dog, released his grip from around my throat, and Andy disappeared.

I rolled around in the morning dew, digging my fingers through pine needles and grass, grabbing for something to help me stand. My grip fell upon a low-hanging branch, but before I could pull myself upright, Meyer punted me in the ribs, and my whole side burst from a shockwave of pain. The current carried my body sideways; I ricocheted off a neighboring pine and fell into a tangle of kudzu. My arms and legs got knotted in the vines, and Meyer came forward, stepped into fading star gleams, and Randy Jessup's face replaced his.

A smirk made a jagged line across the preacher's face, and he stared down at me with two empty sockets; and a pair of coin-colored copperheads slithered out of them, wound their way down his neck and shoulders, and twisted around his arms. Randy Jessup stretched his arms out to their full length, letting the snakes coil around his forearms until their heads rested in his hands. He stood above me now, bent at the waist, opened his mouth to speak, and sounded like a song bell, "Hear these words from the Revelation of Jesus Christ, friend, '*The same shall drink of the wine of the wrath of God, which is poured out without mixture into the cup of his indignation; and he shall be tormented with fire and brimstone in the presence of the holy angels, and in the presence of the Lamb . . .'"*

Randy Jessup stood to his full height, his gravedigger's form slim in the star glow, held a flaming Bible above his head and proclaimed the wrath of God until I jacked my bootheel into his ball sack. Meyer's face came into focus then, his eyes rolled into the back of his head, and he stumbled backward into Peanut's open arms. Peanut ragdolled the man into an oak tree, palmed his face like a basketball and smashed his skull into the trunk. Peanut did that over and over until Meyer's head burst like a melon getting dropped on the floor, and the sound of his head thunking against the tree turned to a wet splat. Peanut didn't stop until his arm gave out, dropped Meyer's body in the grass, and collapsed next to him.

I laid there in those kudzu vines until I got the strength to untangle myself from them and used a low-hanging limb to pull myself upright. It took a few minutes before my legs steadied enough for me to stand without the tree's assistance, but once I could walk, I hiked my way out of the woods, scrambled up the hillside, and flagged down the first truck I saw.

The driver was an old-timer who recognized me because he ran with my Deddy back in the day, but I couldn't put a name to his face, at least not in my beaten state. I asked him for a cell phone, but when he said he didn't carry one, I told him Peanut needed help and to get it here before his condition got serious. The old man hauled ass down the mountainside after I told him who to call, and I stumbled back down the hill, hollering for Otis.

10.

Winter moved into Tugalo County like a bad next-door neighbor, burying the whole world in white fluffs of snow, and freezing temperatures sliced through cloth and bone, cut out my double-wide's power, and froze the water pipes. Jessa and me toughed out the cold for as long as we could by tying our bodies together into impossible knots, piled ourselves under a heap of blankets, and kept a kerosene heater blazing until we ran out of fuel. Mama said we ought to stay at her place where we could run the generator, eat a hot meal, and have some privacy while she shacked with Buford.

Mama's single-wide was only a few minutes ride from where we lived, but I didn't let Jessa's car get above a snail's pace because I couldn't see the ditches for the piles of snow on either side of me, and if the Ford got moving too fast it skidded every time it rolled across a patch of ice. Jessa sat in the passenger's seat, snickering at how I leaned over the steering wheel, hands gripped at ten and two, squinting at the road ahead of me, unable to see where I could turn into Mama's driveway.

I plowed through Mama's yard, churning up a rooster tail of snow behind me, left a path of clean grass for others to use, and parked Jessa's Ford a hop away from the trailer's front door instead of under the carport. Jessa got the keys from me and dove out into the cold to unlock the front door while I hiked around to the generator and got it going. My body shivered all over, and numbness spread through me, hinting at how death might taste.

Andy startled me when I came around the corner, standing knee-deep in the snow, wearing nothing more than a floral print sundress in this cold, showing off all those curves I mapped out in my head. She stared at me with gravestone eyes, still angry I hadn't let Meyer take me from this world. I ignored her presence and got the generator running, leaving her for the warm embrace of the woman I lived with now.

Jessa greeted me at the front door with a towel to stomp my boots off on and said to get out of my clothes.

"Damn, woman, we just now got here."

"Hey, sweetness," she said. "I ain't trying to get you naked. I want you out of them wet clothes so you can change into these." Jessa passed me a pair of Georgia Bulldogs sweatpants and a hoodie for me to wear now. "But if you'll behave, you might get you some later."

I shut the bathroom door, turned on the light, and Andy stood across from me with her shoulders slumped and looked at me with mournful eyes. My visions of her became a constant occurrence after my confrontation with Meyer, alcohol no longer a necessary ingredient for me to conjure her from the otherworld. Andy stayed with me now, judging me for not wanting to join her and attempting to move on with my life. I only did what I thought I should do, and it agitated her spirit in the process, which frustrated me. Andy's pretty eyes filled with resentment for how I loved Jessa, and I tossed my clothes at her for the shame she made me feel. My sweats cut through her form the way fog lights do mist, and she disappeared, leaving me standing in the bathroom alone.

"Good Lord, you look like you done seen a ghost."

Jessa stood at the end of the trailer's short hallway, wearing nothing but a tank top and the shadows around her; her hair fell over her shoulders in waves and hugged the sharp angles of her face.

I stood at the opposite end of the hall, staring at my girlfriend, my mind creating pictures of her I would remember forever, and held back tears.

"You seeing her again?" Jessa's tone didn't change, but I could hear some concern in it.

"When I cranked up the generator and, in the bathroom, just now."

"You need to do what I told you to, Mack." Jessa stood close to me now, leaning against the trailer wall, playing with the hoodie's drawstrings.

"I ain't ready to do that yet."

"It's almost been two years."

"I don't think I can do it, Jessa."

"I said I'd go with you."

"She wouldn't want you there."

"And if it was me, I wouldn't want her there either."

"You ain't making it no better."

Jessa's hand slipped down to mine and pulled me away from the bathroom door. "Well, let's go get under some covers and see if I can't get your mind off of her."

Jessa kept me in bed for the rest of the day, neither of us leaving the tangle of sheets unless it was to go pee. I got up once after my cell phone started ringing and found it in the pocket of my wet jeans. I flipped it open, saw Mama's name on the Caller ID, held the phone to my ear, and said, "Hello."

"You doing all right, son?"

"We're good, Mama. Got to your trailer this morning."

"Generator running okay?"

"Ain't had no problems out of it."

I walked back to the bedroom and got in the bed next to Jessa.

"All right," Mama said. "I just wanted to call and check on yall."

"Hey, Mama, why don't you come stay with me and Jessa."

"I'd rather yall have the privacy, son."

"I just figured you'd like to come stay at your place for a night or two."

"I'm good here with Buford, Mack."

"Mama, you been with him ever since Marshall disappeared."

"I don't wanna be out on these roads, son."

"I'll come get you."

"Mackenzie, I don't want you out on these roads either."

"I don't like you staying with him."

Mama sighed in my ear, and I jerked my arm because Jessa pinched me. I looked over at her, and she mouthed for me to shut up.

I sighed, said, "You heard from Marshall at all?"

"No, I haven't. Have you?"

"No, sure ain't. Don't think either of us will."

"You think he's all right, son?"

"Mama, you know Marshall."

"That's why I asked."

"He'll be fine. Peanut'll make sure of it."

"All right, son. I'm gone letcha go. Love ya."

"Love you too, Mama."

I flipped my phone shut and went to set it on the night-stand next to me when it started ringing again. I flipped it open, saw Monty's name, and said, "What's up, brother?"

"Hey, where you at?"

"We're staying over at Mama's. Ain't got no power at the house."

"Care if I come see ya?"

"Naw, come on, man. I'll get Jessa to fix some coffee."

Monty hung up, saying he'd be right over, and we got out of the bed to get dressed.

"I can't stand Mama staying with that man," I said, pulling my hoodie over my head.

Jessa stood across the bed from me, her face smooth and expressionless. "You'd say that no matter who your mama was staying with."

"That ain't true."

"True as God's word."

"I hate it when you say that."

"You hate it cause I'm right."

"Of all the people she could be with right now, why does it got to be Buford goddamn Bohannon?"

"There ain't no way for me to answer that because I ain't your mama, but if I had to guess, I'd imagine it's cause Buford is available and familiar."

"He's a goddamn backstabber, is what he is."

"Mack, your mama's been alone for half your life; let her have it."

I dropped the subject, knowing there'd be no winning with Jessa, went into the kitchen, and got some coffee started. Jessa came in after me, wearing sweatpants and an

Allman Brothers hoodie she stole from me, asked if I'd like a tomato sandwich, and started slicing up one of her own. I told her I'd wait until after I talked with Monty and took a seat in the living room to wait for him.

I got up from the couch after I saw the headlights of his truck reflecting off the snow, stood at the front door until he got out, and held the door open for him. He came up the front porch steps, hands shoved deep into the pockets of the jacket he wore, kicked his boots off once he got inside, and waved at Jessa. I pointed out the coffee to him, and he went and fixed us both a mug. Monty took his black, and I added a couple of ice cubes to mine.

We sat at the kitchen table with Jessa and didn't speak until Monty stopped shivering. He spoke first. "Hell, if it ain't cold out there, ain't it?"

"I hate this time of year," I said.

"It'll get hot again before you know it."

"I'm ready."

Monty took a sip from his mug, his Tugalo County Titans cap pulled low over his eyes, hiding whatever he had on his mind. After he set his cup down, he sat there staring at it, avoiding whatever he'd come here to talk to me about. I let him have some time to gather his thoughts, looked over at Jessa, and she raised her eyebrows, implying to me that she didn't think Monty was okay.

I started to speak, but Monty looked up, allowing me to see the unease in his eyes for the first time, and he said, "Mack, promise me you won't get pissed off at me."

"Hell, I don't even know what to get pissed off at you for. Other than you out driving in the weather like this."

Monty's foot joggled, shaking the whole table, and chewed on the inside of his mouth. "I wanted to speak with you before you got the chance to hear anything through the grapevine."

"Kinda hard to hear anything when you can't leave the house, bud."

"Yeah, but you might get some phone calls."

"Well, tell me what the hell for. You're starting to get me worried."

"Colquitt County called me, Mack."

I didn't say nothing, not understanding what Monty meant.

"They've offered me a job."

"All right? What kinda job?"

"Mack," Jessa said. "He means *the* job."

"Oh shit." I dropped my hands on the table, and Monty squeezed his eyes shut. "Colquitt asked you to come be the head coach?"

"Yeah," Monty answered, his voice small.

"Why the hell would I get pissed off at that for, man?" I leaned across the table, smacking my best friend on the shoulder. "Colquitt County is the spot. It's what you been busting your ass for."

"I ain't took the job yet."

"Well, you ort to."

"If I do, you won't have a job no more, Mack."

"You fucking serious? You got the chance to go take over Georgia's best high school football program, and you're worried if I'm gone have a job or not?"

"You're my best friend. Have been since junior high."

"What the hell difference does that make?"

"I care about you, man."

"And, shit, I care 'bout you. It's why I'm telling you to take that goddamn job."

"The boosters already got Trell Harris on the phone. They're gone have him come in and take over the team."

"Shit, Trell oughta come in and pick up right where you left off."

"Yeah, but he don't want you, Mack. Done made it loud and clear."

"Monty, I don't give a damn, man. We both know there ain't no career for me coaching high school football. I did it cause it was fun working with my best friend."

Monty sat up; his eyes were still uneasy but not over how I'd react. "You really think I oughta take this job?"

"Hell yeah, man. The Dawgs'll have you on the phone in no time."

11.

After the roads cleared and the temperatures outside started rising, Jessa told me she needed to get out of Tugalo County for a few days, wanted to see her mama in Gatlinburg, and asked if I'd care to come. I'd gotten my old job back at the woodworking factory, building antique-style furniture, and didn't need to take time off after just getting back on. Jessa said she'd get back before the weekend and for me not to get too wild without her.

Toward the middle of the week, after I'd done clocked out, my nose was jammed with sawdust, and I couldn't hear nothing but the table saw buzzing in my head—I got in my truck to make a long-overdue visit—but I got partway home when my cell phone started ringing. I dug it out of my pocket, flipped it open to see Peanut's name on the Caller ID, and debated on whether or not I should answer it. I knew he would just call back if I didn't, so I held it to my ear and said, "Hello?"

"Sorry for calling out of the blue like this, Mack."

The voice speaking to me on the other end of the line didn't belong to Peanut, and my brain got confused trying to place it.

"Katie? Everything all right?"

"Yeah, nothing too serious is the matter. It's just one of those things where I didn't know who else to call."

I let my truck roll over to the shoulder of the road and shifted into park. I sat there waiting for Katie to go on, but when she didn't, I asked, "What you needing?"

A stretch of silence filled the distance between us, and when Katie finally broke it, she did so with a wearisome sigh. "This is awkward to have to ask, Mack, and if you don't wanna help me out at all, I totally understand, but I really didn't know who else I could call."

"Katie, you know I'll help you out however I can."

"Peanut's gone, Mack. Ain't been home for days. I think I know where's he's at, but if I show up there looking for him, he'll just holler for me to get back home."

"What the hell you mean he ain't been home?"

"He ain't been right since yall had that wreck. Can't hardly sleep and stays mad all the time."

"That don't sound like him at all."

"It ain't."

"Where can I find him at, Katie?"

After she told me, I made a horseshoe turn and headed toward Blackwood, not knowing what in the world was wrong with Peanut or how I could even help him. I watched the sunset on my way out to where Katie said she thought he'd be, saw the sky turn the color of squash, and reckoned I wouldn't get to make my visit tonight. I cruised the Due South's parking lot, spotted Peanut's new truck parked close to the bar, found me a spot not too far from it, and went inside looking for him.

The Due South had always been a dingy little drinking spot, where cigarette smoke clouded the room, the liquor was plentiful, and the girls were available. Sometimes they got live music here but didn't have any tonight. Country-pop blared from the speaker system, and the Kermit-sounding singer sang about tailgates and dirt roads and girls drinking beer. The scene surrounding me reflected what I heard playing in the bar and is one I would've wanted to be a part of until Jessa became a ball and chain around my ankle, anchoring me to a settled life. In the midst of the hellraisers and the trailer park beauty queens, I saw Peanut bellied up to the bar—his brawny arms hugged around a half-full pint of beer with Otis laying at his feet.

I elbowed my way across the dance floor, getting cussed out for catching folks in the ribs, and took a young lady sitting with Peanut by the elbow, helped her off her barstool, and said, "This seat's occupied."

She looked at me with hazy eyes and took her time speaking, careful not to trip over her words. "Only cause I been sitting here from the time he sat down." She hitched a thumb toward Peanut, him not even bothering to look over.

"Oh well," I said, turning her away from us. "There's some spots over there you can take."

"Well, who the hell—"

"Get the fuck outta here 'fore you walk away wearing that beer."

My threat sobered her up on the spot, and the bartender came over asking if there was a problem. I gave the stout man a once over, said, "Not if you mind your own goddamn business."

The man hesitated, took a moment to evaluate my seriousness, and said, "Hey, Angie, come on over here and leave these boys alone. I gotcha one on the house."

Angie sauntered off, enough alcohol already circulating through her system to make each slow step deliberate and necessary. I slid onto the seat next to Peanut, reached down to Otis, scratched him between the ears, and said, "I don't think you're allowed to have dogs in here."

Peanut turned his head in my direction, squinting at me through fuzzy eyes. "I know you were thinking something was fixing to happen between me and that girl, but that ain't some shit I would do to Katie. You've knowed me long enough to know that."

"I wasn't thinking shit, Peanut."

"You came off awful hateful."

"Only cause this's about the last damn place I wanna be."

"It is a shit hole, ain't it?"

"Ain't never been nothing else."

After the bartender got Angie settled, he came back over, rested soft hands on the bar, and spoke with deference, "Would ya like a drink, bud? First round's on me as long as there ain't gone be no trouble."

"Woodford on the rocks," I said without checking my brain.

Peanut glanced over at me, took a long swig of his beer, licked the suds from his mustache, said, "What the hell's done got into you?"

"Nothing. Just answered outta reflex."

"Well, hell, tell him you changed yer mind. Get a Co-Cola."

"I'll be fine."

Peanut sat up tall on his barstool, squared his shoulders, grabbed his beer, chugged what was left, burped, and said, "Now, I done got too drunk to break up any fights you get yerself into tonight, Mack. Have yer drink and then don't have no more after that, you hear me?"

"I don't need you to mama me around, Peanut."

"I ain't trying to mama you around. I'm looking out for my best interest."

"If that's so, why're you here?"

Peanut cocked his head sideways, said, "What's that supposed to mean?"

The bartender brought me a plastic cup piled high with ice with a watered-down three-finger pour of Woodford Reserve. I lifted the cup to my mouth, took a long sniff of the drink; the ethanol woke my senses up, and sipped. My tongue savored the burn, enjoying the blend of vanilla and honey and orange peel and rye and oak. I sat the cup down, pushed it out of reach, hating to waste good alcohol, and said, "That right there will get me in some goddamn trouble."

"Damn, if that ain't right."

I turned to Peanut, laying a heavy gaze on him. "Katie says you ain't been home for days."

"I knew that's why you're here."

"Well, what the hell, Peanut? You got her worried sick."

Peanut reached across the bar, took my cup of Woodford in hand, slurped it down, and started chomping ice.

"She said you ain't been yourself since the wreck."

Peanut shrugged.

"Listen here, Jessa's outta town, and I ain't got no plans tonight. I'll sit here 'til your fat-ass talks, by God."

Peanut waved the bartender over, pointed at the plastic cup, said, "Another one of those."

The bartender grabbed a bottle and poured until Peanut said for him to stop. Peanut drained the bourbon and pounded his chest after it burned its way through him. "I'm scared to death, Mack." He spoke low, his voice faint, almost soundless compared to the music. "Everything that happened with Kendall and yer brother and the Ghostface

Devils has got me questioning whether or not I should be involved in this life anymore. I damn near got my family killed, man. My wife and my boys. You know what it would do to me if I had to bury a single one of 'em? It'd be over for me, son. I'd drive myself all the way to the top of Albermarle Mountain and throw myself over the fucking side. I can't stand to look at 'em right now. I can't see nothing but tombstones."

"Then get out," I said. "You got the means to do it. Get out and get the fuck outta here, Peanut. Don't ever come back. It don't matter where you go neither. Take Katie and Riley and Ramsey and Ray, and do something better for 'em."

Peanut stared at me, his chest ballooning and deflating with tears welling in his eyes but never running down his cheeks. He pointed at his cup again, and the bartender came from the opposite end of the bar and poured until Peanut gave him a thumbs up. This time, Peanut didn't drink. He let the bourbon sit while he stared into a sign's neon glow.

After a time, with his bourbon left untouched and my ass sore from sitting so long, Peanut thumped me on the back and spoke like nothing was ever the matter with him, "Care if I crash at yer place tonight? I'm seeing three of everything and don't know which way to fucking go."

12.

The next morning, I woke up early, rinsed myself off under icy water, and left my double-wide with Peanut and Otis still sleeping on the couch. It was chilly outside from winter's dying grip still clutching the world, but spring was starting to bloom—green grass flattened under my bootheels, leaves had begun filling tree branches, and the sky looked a little extra blue. I got in my truck and aimed it toward town.

The Ingles wasn't too busy this early in the day. Parents were dropping their kids off at school, and those who weren't already at work were either still in bed or just getting there. I walked into the grocery store and made my way over to the floral department, where a young lady arranged bouquets. She smiled at me and asked if I could use any help.

"I'm visiting a friend and wanna take her some flowers," I said. "I ain't sure what to pick out here."

"Just a friend?" The girl winked.

"Yes, ma'am. Just a friend."

She spun on her heel, a fingertip stabbing the dimple in her chin while considering the selection of flowers. "How good a friend?" She asked from the corner of her mouth.

"Good enough."

She looked at me sideways. "You're not very helpful."

"It's a girl I used to date," I sighed. "We got some unfinished business."

"Oh," she nodded. "What kind?"

"I need to say goodbye."

I hopped into the cab of my truck, sat a tulip arrangement in the passenger's seat, and spun the radio dial until I found an old country station. Randy Travis sang how his love was deeper than the holler, and I turned the radio off, merging into traffic. I avoided Tugalo County's main roads, not wanting to get stuck behind any school drop-off lines. After I crossed into Blackwood, my palms got sweaty, and a knot started twisting around my stomach.

Calvary Baptist Church sat atop a hill, its driveway a steep climb until it wound around the building and led to a sprawling cemetery behind it. I parked a short walk from the cemetery's entrance and stared at the youth building in my rearview mirror. My parents were never church-going people, but Mama would send me and my brother to their Vacation Bible School to get a break from us during the summertime.

It's where I met Andy.

Her eyes were the first thing I noticed. I caught her looking at me from across the gymnasium, her pupils glimmering the way a pair of diamond earrings do when they would catch the right light. I left whatever game I was playing, ignoring Marshall when he asked where I was going, and went to introduce myself. Andy blushed, told me what school she went to, and asked if I wanted to partner up on this game with her.

We were inseparable for the rest of the summer. She invited me over for pool parties, out to the movies, to Six

Flags over Georgia, and came with me to her first Atlanta Braves game. We held hands but never kissed. She said her deddy told her eleven was too young to go around kissing boys, and she'd get warts if she did. I tried convincing her no such thing would happen, but she was afraid of getting warts.

After summer ended and school got back in, we didn't see each other as much. We didn't have any middle school classes together, and our lunch periods were never the same. Once we got home, we'd talk on the phone until her parents yelled for her to do her homework or unplugged the line. We'd get to school early to see each other before homeroom and would sneak kisses after school. She never did get any warts.

I couldn't recall a single memory from my youth that Andy wasn't a part of. She cheered in the stands the first time I ever hit a home run, was there with my mama after I got carted off the football field with a broken foot, and came to Atlanta when I won state in wrestling. We went to prom together, lost our virginity to each other, and dreamed about getting married. It all fizzled out after high school, and none of those dreams came true.

I pried myself from the seat of my truck, the day seeming hotter now, although the temperature hadn't changed. Sweat beaded across my forehead, my clothes clung to my arms and the backs of my legs, and I got lightheaded standing before the cemetery entrance. Hills rolled with tombstones and grave markers, going on until my eyes strained to see them. I unlatched the gate and forced my body into movement, stepping into a world of mourning.

Angelic monuments escorted me along the graveyard's footpath, and weathered headstones told me the story of those who rested here. Some dated back to before the Civil

War, and others came to lie in their graves only weeks ago. Children and adults and babies and mothers and fathers and sons and daughters all occupied this place. Some were wives, and some were husbands. Some lay alone, waiting for their significant other to join them here in this eternal place of rest.

I hiked over a hill and came to stand near a row of evergreens. Andy waited for me at the end of them. She stood there wearing a dress with a bright floral print, cut off at her knees, and she wore sandals on her feet, her toes painted the color of summer. Her eyes sparkled when she saw me—like stars do on a clear August night. A smile stretched across her face, tugging at my heart the way it always did.

My feet moved without any assistance from my brain, each step bringing me closer to the source of my mourning. Andy held her hands in front of her, her fingers intertwined, not a single muscle twitching. Her eyes gave off a light of their own now, and her smile tugged me into another world. We stood together in a room where pictures of us hung on the walls. Each photograph was a memory I'd brought to mind before getting out of my truck. I looked each one over, remembering every moment's detail until my eyes met Andy's, and I handed the tulips over. She reached out for them, took the arrangement from me, and held it to her nose.

Andy's eyes closed, and she inhaled until the grassy green fragrance of the tulips filled her lungs, and she opened her eyes again, staring at me over the petals.

"I'm sorry," I said, speaking to her for the first time since she'd left my world.

Andy brought the tulip arrangement from her face, letting them rest at her hip. "Why ain't you come to see me?"

I shook my head.

"I've been waiting on you, Mack. I've been restless."

Tears welled in my eyes, but I held them back.

"Being here is hard. I have to watch you live without me, and you won't even acknowledge that I'm gone."

"I don't want to let you go." My voice strained, the way a muscle does when it exerts too much force.

"And I don't wanna let you go, but I got to now."

I bit my cheek, doing my best not to cry.

"You can't keep me in your world. You got to let me go."

"I don't know how."

"You gotta tell me goodbye, Mack."

"Andy."

"Please."

"I don't want to."

Her smile went flat, and the sparkles left her eyes. "It ain't your fault, Mack."

"Don't say that."

"I already did."

"Well, I can't believe it."

"Don't make it untrue."

I stood across from her, my legs stiff and hands shaking. I reached into a pocket and fumbled with a box I debated on bringing. Her eyes went to it, and some of the sparkles returned.

"When did you get her that?"

I opened the box, showing Andy the diamond.

"It's pretty," Andy said. "She'll love it."

"I don't know how to give it to her."

"You do. You're just scared."

"I'm afraid if I give it to her, I'll lose you forever."

Andy came forward in a blink, her eyes flashing and bright. She placed a hand on my cheek, her touch soft and consoling, her thumb brushing my skin. I squeezed my eyes shut until I thought they might burst and let everything out when she said it was okay. All the tears I'd dammed up inside me came out in a rush. My wails surged from my lungs, and my body quaked from weeping. My arms embraced Andy, pressing her into my chest, hoping I could make us one. I hugged her that way until her headstone replaced her body, and I squeezed it to me until my arms got tired, and I had no choice but to let her go.

ACKNOWLEDGMENT

N ot every writer gets the chance to publish once. Even fewer get the opportunity to publish twice. This second book wouldn't be in your hands right now without the help and guidance of Ron Earl Phillips.

Ron, you believed in the Dooley brothers before anyone else got to read word one of *A Violent Gospel*. I appreciate you trusting me to build their world and allowing me to experiment and take chances with how I tell their stories. And if I've said it once, then I've said it 875,963 times, nobody else has got the magic when it comes to designing covers that you do. Well done, man. Every time!

I can't write these acknowledgments without mentioning my writing buddies, Scott Blackburn, Brodie Lowe, Bobby Mathews, and JB Stevens. If every writer had a group of friends like this, then none of us would ever be struggling with impostor syndrome. I can always count on these men to push and challenge me to leave blood on every page. They also keep me off my bullshit, which is important if you know me.

This edition to the Dooley Brothers Universe is probably not the same story that it is without J. Todd Wilkins putting ideas in my head. When I wasn't sure where the

Dooley brothers should go next he acted as a sounding board for me and helped me map out the plans for Mack and Marshall's next adventure.

As always, thank you to each author who said kind things about this book. You're each master storytellers in your own right and should all be household names.

Finally, to Dawn. Every word I write belongs solely to you. Love you!

Mark Westmoreland is a Georgia native who lives in Oklahoma with his wife and two dogs. He's a full-time Dawgs fan with a sideline as a writer. Sippin' bourbon and watching Burt Reynolds are two of his favorite pastimes. He is the author of *A Violent Gospel* and *A Mourning Song*. You can find him hanging out on Twitter @ItsMarkYall.

2012 • 2022

CELEBRATING 10 YEARS OF
FICTION WITH A KICK

THE ROAD IS JUST BEGINNING
shotgunhoneybooks.com

CPSIA information can be obtained
at www.ICGtesting.com
Printed in the USA
LVHW092114160922
728592LV00010B/705